MICHAEL J. ARBOUET

GODS

Eliana Soleil
PUBLISHING

Eliana Soleil Publishing

Originally published in paperback by Eliana Soleil Publishing

ISBN: 978-1-7323223-0-1

eBook ISBN: 978-1-7323223-8

Printed in the United States of America

www.mikearbouet.com

Eliana Soleil Publishing mass market edition: September 2018

This book is dedicated to my wife Cheryl and my girls Leila and Sahara, for the late nights, finger pokes in the face and silly dances.

PROLOGUE

We forget. No matter what we do as a people time has a way of erasing our collective memories. So, things that we need to remember get lost in the great lake of time, like a water droplet gets lost in a pond. No matter what we do, we omit our history; it slips through our fingers like sand. History becomes legend and legend becomes folklore and what we should know is forgotten. Our elders-built cities and wrote the secrets down, so we would always remember.

A thousand years passed, and the cities were taken back by the earth and the language was forgotten. We lost the ability to read what was written. The great cycle births us; we grow, become great, we are tested. If we fail, all is lost, and we must begin again.

This is how it has been from the beginning. We have a nasty habit of trying to destroy each other. We have gotten very good at war. At first it was tribe against tribe with the victor taking what they wanted. Then the fight was nation against nation. Our weapons got better. Thousands perished, then tens of thousands. The world we knew was on the brink of destruction.

Our elders ban the use of our natural abilities. Those touched with the "gifts" went into hiding a stalemate was reached and there was peace for thousands of years. Even with the great statutes we built, the pyramids and monuments to help us remember, we forgot. We forgot the horror of war and fought among ourselves once more.

First, we fought for land, then we fought for the gods, when the gods did not answer us, we fought for our ideals, if your belief differed from what another believed that was all that was needed to fight and so we did fight and created horrible weapons, terrible weapons and somehow, we developed the power to destroy the entire world. However, we forgot about the cycle. It is time. It is time to either be reborn to this world or disappear forever.

CHAPTER ONE

Crackpots and conspiracy theorists are the only ones that had a permanent setup at Devil's Fork nowadays. When the Fork was first created over 10 years ago, every news agency from around the globe had claimed a spot near it...and they waited and watched, ready to report.

They ran stories about its creation and the possible effect it would have on the environment. Then there were those brave souls who tried to explore the Fork but lost their lives due to the hurricane-force winds in the canyon.

Every airship you can imagine has been smashed and torn to pieces. The wreckage was strewn in every direction for miles and served as a deadly reminder that death is the only thing you will find if you try to enter. Rufus enjoyed his little game of hide-and-seek with border patrol; they had to try to make it appear as if they were doing their job, after all.

They mostly chased away scavengers looking for scrap metal to sell—the only thing of value around. It was easy enough for Rufus to drive his tiny house around until dark, then find a nice secluded spot to park and live stream his show "Tenedor del Diablo." He had a good five-thousand-plus followers, and their donations allowed him to live his nomadic lifestyle.

Because of his rail thin body frame, Rufus resembled Shaggy from Scooby-Doo. But that's where the comparisons end. He was known for his signature pair of circular-frame eyeglasses, made famous by Beatles' front man John Lennon. The spectacles also highlighted his stunning emerald green eyes, which were only magnified for full display by the glass in the frame. His dazzling peepers were popular with the ladies. And he knew it. Only two percent of the world's population had green eyes, and he often used this fact as an icebreaker when meeting new people. He was shy around people he didn't know especially men, but it was that quirky shyness that made him attractive to women. Apart from his sparkling emerald orbs, his fashion sense also made him stand out to the opposite sex. Let's face it, the hipster is just a poor man's version of the American metrosexual instead of fitted suits in his closet, there was a multitude of multicolor sweatshirts, of which he dons an almost-endless stockpile, to the 90s relic Dr. Martens sandals he wore while sneaking around the Fork. There was something alluring about his geek chic that couldn't be denied. It was something people who met him found strange because of all the followers he had on social media but then again that's an oxymoron because in truth there is nothing really social about it. He didn't know most of the people who followed him and his work.

His 300-square-foot mobile abode was perfect for the nomadic lifestyle popular among his age group. He loved being able to pick up and just move at a moment's notice. Rufus took the concept of minimalist living and combined it with smart technology. The result? Rufus lives better than the generation before him—debt-free and seeing more of the United States than his parents, or even his grandparents, ever had. Although small, his space was tricked out with smart doors and locks, high-tech solar panels, a retractable deck and roof, as well as voice-operated lights and air conditioning. His residence did double duty, as it was also his office. He was able to do freelance work from anywhere, with time to spare for his video podcast passion project.

Rufus found a nice secluded spot and parked his pygmy cottage-on-wheels in the shadows of some large trees. Only half way through his burrito, he took one more massive bite and used a napkin to wipe the bean and sour cream remnants from the corners of his mouth. He got out of the driver's seat of his truck and disconnected it from the trailer hitch attachment.

Once his residence was secured, Rufus opened the front door and walked to the back to get ready for his weekly podcast live stream.

While waiting for the computer to warm up, he grabbed a pint-sized palm camera, complete with tripod, and climbed the stairs to his loft. Looking up at the ceiling above his bed was a hatchway that led to the rooftop deck.

Rufus ascended to the open-air perch and let the warm summer air fill his lungs. The Fork's powerful winds could still be felt from that distance, forcing the podcaster to brace himself while setting up his gear.

Using his smartphone as a controller, he adjusted the camera for low-light settings. Firmly pressing his thumb to the "live" icon, the phone blinked a red beam to indicate he was good to go.

Rufus spoke animatedly at the camera. "Greeting and Salutations Forkers!" Rufus chuckled at his own joke. "The rest of the world has gone back to their boring mundane lives, but not us, not the true believers. This, this is something incredible! After all this time, no one knows what secrets the Fork holds!" The Great Quake reshaped the fucking continent! The Quake created Woati Island and they want to become their own sovereignty!"

Rufus leans in closer to the camera as if he is going to tell his best friend a secret. He whispered, "Something big is going to happen soon! I can fucking feel it!" A rumble low and growing louder can be heard in the distance. Rufus turns around just in time to see a rocket come flying out of Devil's Fork.

Excitedly, Rufus turned back towards the camera yelling. "Holy Shit! Did you all see that! I can't believe it! A rocket just came flying out of the Fork! I don't know if this is an attack or what?"

Rufus grabs the camera off the tripod and points it towards the sky. He speaks more to himself than his audience. "Look at that thing go!" At about 60 or 70 feet in the air, Rufus temporarily loses sight of the rocket.

He pans the camera left and right trying to catch sight of it. "Something is happening! Did it blow up?" Again, posing the question more to himself than his audience, his eyes finds the rocket and he yells out. "It's deploying a parachute!" It's floating back down!"

Rufus pointed the camera at himself, causing his face to look large and distorted to those watching the stream. "We have to see where that thing lands! I don't think it's a weapon! It might be a beacon or there might be something inside from..."

Rufus quickly looks up and gathers his thoughts before going back through the hatch to his loft. The image on the camera shakes, which he knows must be dizzying to anyone tuned in.

On a mission to pinpoint the cause of the recent commotion, Rufus secures his camera to the suction-cup mounting on the truck before hopping in the driver's seat.

With camera pointed at himself, Rufus drives onto a dirt road and exclaims in to the lens, "The rocket is towards the north east, floating down towards the left side of the Fork!"

Although the rocket looks like it is falling gently towards the earth, it is actually falling at around 25 miles per hour. Rufus looks to his left. "We are about to go off road people!" he yells as he turns the wheel, making a sharp turn onto the bumpy terrain.

At about the 70 feet away from his position, the rocket hits the ground just in front of his vehicle. Rufus skids to a stop and looks at his camera. "I can't believe this! A rocket just flew out of the Fork and has just landed a couple of feet away from me! We are the very first to see this, people!"

Rufus unhooks the camera from the dashboard mount and gets out of the truck and runs towards the rocket. Out of breath, Rufus reaches the rocket. Pointing the camera at it, he speaks to his audience, "It's a plane. There are no markings I can see on it, but there is still quite a bit of heat coming from it."

Rufus turns the camera towards himself to address his fans, behind him a figure in a black military uniform lifts a sub machine gun up and strikes Rufus in the back of his head. Everything goes dark.

CHAPTER TWO

Devil's Fork is a buzz with activity. Three days ago, all was silent. Not now, thanks to the wonderful advances in technology news no longer takes days or hours but seconds to travel.

A podcast by Rufus Bartlett went viral and what was old is now new again. Devil's Fork is now on the lips of anyone with a computer, television and radio. News both confirmed and unconfirmed has been flowing out of Devil's Fork for days.

The headlines change every couple of minutes from the disappearance of Rufus Bartlett and what happened to him, to possible alien UFO's being spotted in the area. WWN the World-Wide News Network broke the story forty-eight hours ago that the rocket seen flying out of Devil's Fork may have been sent by two relatively unknown research assistants working for Berkeley University under Doctor Russell Kaplan.

According to previous podcast by Bartlett the two research assistants were seen studying Devil's Fork, taking soil samples.

A makeup artist quickly worked on reporter Nancy Epstein's hair and make-up as a camera was being set up near Devil's Fork. She lifted the microphone up to her lips, the logo for the World-Wide News Network can be clearly seen. The cameraman signals to her with a hand gestures indicating that they are now broadcasting live, Nancy began her report.

"Sixteen months ago, scientist Michael McLoughlin and Keith Weber have been studying the seismic activity in the region which has been on going for the past five years. Who would have thought that two weeks ago the team would come back with the possible discovery of a lost world?

A shift in the earth's crust formed a huge chasm. Most of the world won't forget the day when South America was hit with the worst earthquake ever recorded in the world's history registering a frightening 10.5 causing massive devastation like the destruction of the Panama Canal and the creation of Woati Island.

The quake was so massive that the shock waves were felt throughout North America. The canyon which is now known as Devil's Fork is one quarter bigger than the Grand Canyon and runs an estimated 6,454 miles below sea level.

Until just recently exploring the canyon was an impossibility because of the massive tornado winds that is created within the canyon.

Some winds blowing at 415 miles per hour made any attempt to fly into the fork a suicide mission. As you can see airplane and helicopter wreckage is strewn all over the area.

So how did the two scientists get in to the fork? That is being kept a secret by the American Government until further research can be made.

If one were to look at the wreckage along the canyon it would look like the garbage dump for the United Nations. Just about every country in the world has tried to gain access to the canyon and failed. Which is why for the past eighteen months the United Nations has also been making headlines."

CHAPTER THREE

The UN has some fundamental strengths and weaknesses that handicap getting anything done. The idea is that if every country can get together they can make the world a better place.

Its legitimacy comes from the fact that every country is a member and feels it has a voice. Today however, The UN Security Council squabble and argue like a bunch of teenagers watching a heated football match, everyone being keen to add their own point of view. Jeffrey wasn't ready to go back into the room.

He was tired, physically and mentally drained. Usually the sessions were never this bad; he wondered if this is how Iran or China must feel when the other powers ganged up against them.

As the representative for the United States of America he had never been in this position and he didn't like it. He stood in the small private bathroom looking at his reflection for a long moment. "I'm getting older" he thought to himself as he looked at yet more graying hair that seemed to appear from nowhere on top of his head. Jeffrey looked like he was manufactured in his voice, manners and features, his face was forgettable. He was a mid-aged man of ordinary build. The only thing that set him apart from the masses was the intelligence you could see in his muddy brown eyes. It was his eyes that allowed him to quell the storms of angry words or have you believe that the tooth fairy was real. His eyes in combination with his deep baritone voice had the power to stop wars or seduce women or men whatever your fancy might be.

He washed his tired looking face in an attempt to reinvigorate himself. It didn't work. Drying his face, he took a deep breath and stepped out of the bathroom.

Jeffrey walked down a long hallway until he reached two guards that stood by a metal detector. Jeffrey nodded to one of the guards who recognized him. "Back at it sir?" Jeffery smiled. "Yep, getting ready for round three." Jeffrey walked through the detector without incident and opened one of the two large double doors.

The main room is massive, big enough to hold hundreds of people, with a separate section for the press and special guests. If this were a general assembly there would be one hundred and ninety-three countries represented, today however is just a meeting with the Security Council comprised of only 15 members.

The five permanent members included France, China, the Russian Federation, the United Kingdom and the United States of America.

The ten non-permanent members of the Security Council are elected every two years. As Jeffery makes his way to the circular table that looks like a giant letter "C" the rest of the Security Council take their seats and a hush falls across the room.

Rajendra Mehta the ambassador from India begins the discussions, quickly going on the attack as she speaks to Jeffery.

"We should all be working together as a team to explore this new world. Instead you have done what all Americans have done for the past 100 years which is rape mother earth of all her gifts! India will not stand for it! You have no right to stop any of the other countries from the peaceful exploration of this new world!"

Jeffrey Houston made no attempt to bite back. He looked around the room and managed to sneak out a cocky but thin smile across his lips.

The woman sounded bitter. She always did, and Jeffery hated having to deal with her but there was no choice obviously. To make things worse, the room had erupted into a raucous cheer of clapping for the Indian Ambassador. Her support mainly came from the third world countries.

Jeffrey rested his elbows on the table and watched them like hawks would do their prey. He was an American after all, and he wouldn't be bullied.

"You all don't seem to be getting my point," he said with some frustration. "I repeat, we have no intent in stopping anyone who has been cleared to explore this new world which so happens to be on the United States of America's soil."

His words rang sighs and hisses from the discontent people.

"From all we know, nothing is understood about how to really get into that canyon and it would be foolish to waste our lives and resources until we do so," Jeffery continued with a sigh. "This isn't some journey into the Bahamas, or sea exploration. This is more delicate, and we cannot-."

He had hoped to continue when the man with the thickest beard in the room interjected in aggression.

"You are not the great super power you once where Mr. Houston we all have the power to destroy if need be. You won't rob us of our right to mine the untapped natural resources in the canyon or try to destroy us by weakening the market!" Mr. Sudan, the Iranian Ambassador spat out.

Jeffrey was at a loss for words before the Ambassador for England picked up from where the Iranian Ambassador had left off. Eugene Tepper was someone Jeffrey had been hoping would see reason with him on the subject matter of blindly sending in people to their possible deaths into a situation they still knew nothing about. The idea of opening the canyon for anyone and everyone from other countries to fly into without control could be disastrous, if not come to haunt them again since they still couldn't figure out how to get into the canyon safely.

Tepper looked at Jeffrey with pleading eyes. "We all want economic stability Mr. Sudan however as much as I hate to admit this Jeff, it does appear that the US has the advantage in this situation. We can all watch the telly to see the World-Wide News report that McLoughlin and Weber have finally entered the fork. Frankly I feel that if the news reports are true it should have been a joint effort."

Tepper was playing it smart. He was being a diplomat and Jeffery could smell his bullshit from afar, so he remained silent. Also, the room had calmed down and lowered the air of rage it had when the Indian Ambassador first spoke.

The hostility had dampened, and Jeffrey Houston could now permit himself to stand before them all to speak. He unbuttoned his suit and placed both hands on the table for support while he leaned forward. The eyes staring right back at him were beckoning with hopes for some enticing information.

"I can relate with your feelings," Jeff finally spoke and cleared his throat.

Some whispers intended at declining the fact in his words momentarily aired but he paid no attention to them.

"To place your minds at rest, yes, some of the reports you heard are true," he confessed. "Before I continue let me remind you that what I'm about to tell you doesn't leave this room. I must insist on Alpha security."

It was the protocol required when handling sensitive information. Upon the other members agreeing, a glass dome automatically descended from above enclosing them in a soundproof sphere. From somewhere in the room a white noise generator came on. Noise generators help protect private conversations with out the other party's knowledge. Its inaudible to humans but scrambles microphones. Jeffrey Houston waited for the "safe" light indicator to switch on before doing anything.

It finally came on and he began explaining after some brief seconds had passed. The Ambassadors looked impatient and he could not blame them. He truly had been sitting on information he would kill to have had he been the one in their shoes.

"As you have heard McLoughlin and Weber have entered the canyon. We assumed that they were dead because all attempts to enter the canyon failed. Apparently the two men created a ship of their own design to enter the canyon. That was two months ago. This morning at about 3:30am a small rocket came flying out of the canyon. The media saw this and made their own conclusions. This digital recording is the only reasons why we know there alive," Jeffrey Houston explained.

He held the recorder in his hand for them to see. He made certain that everyone got a good glimpse of it before he placed it on the table.

"This recording is the only evidence we have to tell that they are indeed alive," Jeffrey spoke without being interrupted.

He picked up the digital recorder and clicked on the "play button" while everyone listened on. The first voice to play out was that of Keith Weber.

KEITH WEBER;

Uh… Hello this is Keith Weber and I am here with my friend and colleague Michael McLoughlin. It is about 9:37 a.m. We are making history here. We have successfully traveled to the bottom of the canyon. It took 15 days, but we made it! There is so much to tell you Professor Russ —

MICHAEL MCLOUGHLIN;

What Keith is trying to say is that the discovery we have made today makes the Apollo moon-landing look like a kindergarten school trip. We have only been here for five hours and have already discovered eight new animal species, or old species depending on how you look at it. During our brief stay here, we have encountered what looks like a saber tooth tiger.

We would have told you about the ship, but we had to keep it a secret. We want to bring back the knowledge of this place first before the world goes and pollutes this as well. I really hope that you get this message. As you can see we have sent something back to show you how valuable this place is. Show this to the nations of the world tell them this place is special and not to be touched or mined at least until we have a better understanding of it. We will try to contact you in twenty-nine days.

Good-bye.

The digital recorder popped with static feedback for the next few seconds before stopping. Jeffery walked over to the Alpha mode button to switch it off. He waited for the noise-cancelling generator to shut off and the dome to lift before they would continue the business of the day.

Hong-Zen Cho, the Japanese Ambassador addressed Jeffery. "What came with the recording?"

It was the question on all their lips, and he wasn't surprised.

Jeffrey looked around the room momentarily before pushing a button by his side of the table, some armed guards came into the room carrying a large covered cage. The black cloth provided no hint of what lurked underneath it. Their attention remained solely on the large cage just as Jeffrey yanked off the black covering like a magician would do for effect.

Within the confinement of the cage was a creature that resembled a small ferret. It had large, multicolored wings on its back, and the audience stared in bewilderment and awe. They were struck with the desire to know what they were looking at and the fire burning in their eyes, aching for knowledge was precisely what Jeffery had expected.

For the first time in the day, the United Nations meeting room fell silent in genuine accordance. The odd creature let out a cry resembling that of a young woman's voice holding the "A" chord for a moment. Jeffrey smiled to himself cockily. Deep down he knew this would be as close as they would get to the secrets of the fork but no further.

CHAPTER FOUR

Location; Egypt- Desert

Roland hated having to explain what he did for a living. Most people thought he was a polyglot. A polyglot is someone who speaks many different languages and usually finds work as an interpreter or a language teacher.

Although its true Roland can speak a number of languages, sixty-seven to be exact not many people knows this about him, he didn't want to be considered a circus freak or end up in the Guinness book of World Records.

If memory serves him correctly the previous record holder speaks fifty-two languages but to his credit the other languages Roland is fluent in are considered dead languages and not many people speak or even know of their existence.

Roland is a linguist. The study of the structure of language and communication as a whole is what Roland loved. It is his absolute passion.

The acoustics of speech and how it sounds to the ear, the structure of words and structure of sentences and their meaning, it was a lovely puzzle for Roland to put together. He could mentally take languages apart and put them back together in his mind.

Many of his colleagues thought he might be and idiot savant, a vulgar French term used to describe an autistic savant, they simply could not grasp his ability of how he is able to grasp language so quickly, after a day of hearing a language spoken, Roland had no trouble speaking the language in its basic form and will become completely fluent in about a week's time, he will also be able to write and read in that language as well.

Roland has a form of synesthesia where the letters and symbols take various textures and hues in colors that aid him when he manipulates the language in order to understand it.

Trying to describe this to other people was always frustrating so after a couple of years he gave up trying. If Roland had to be described perhaps he is a prodigious savant of language.

He is to his knowledge the only one in the world who can do what he can do. So, when he got the call to fly half way around the world to examine what could be a lost form of language, he jumped at the chance to be the first to see it.

What he didn't count on was having to be in this unbearable heat and the smell. Roland was riding on the back of a camel in the middle of the desert following a guide to God knows where.

The ride itself was surprising smooth, sitting in the saddle you sway back and forth almost as if the animal was trying to rock the rider to sleep.

I imagine it's because when a camel walks, they move their right two legs then their left two legs a lot different than a horse's gait, however like birds, camels regurgitated their food, when they burp up the slimy half-digested food, it literally smells like shit.

The smell was turning Roland stomach and it didn't help when he had to take a drink of water to stay hydrated. So, it was a relief when Roland saw tents rising up from the horizon off in the distance, how long will it take to get there he wondered until he saw a jeep speeding dangerously in his direction as if it intended to run him and his foul-smelling camel down. The camel bellowed and grunted sounding like an off key ancient blowing horn, seeming to sense the impending danger. The jeep then swerved a mere ten yards away kicking sand up into the air. A woman dressed in a long sleeve shirt, pants and lightweight hiking boots stepped out of the driver seat. A tan brimmed Tilley hat adorned her head. Dark sport glasses covered her eyes and a bandanna was draped around her neck. That little maneuver not only scared his camel but him as well. He was suddenly aware of his heart beating hard and fast in his chest. The woman stared at Roland a moment before walking up to him, stretching her hand towards him, she intended to help Roland down from his camel. Roland ignored her hand and dismounted the camel himself.

"Dr. Roland Misthos, I presume," she said.

The famous greeting used by Henry Morton Stanley when he located Doctor David Livingstone in Africa wasn't lost on him, he got the joke.

Dr. Misthos waited for the woman who knew his name to introduce herself. The woman took her sunglasses off allowing Roland to see her full face. She spoke with a smile in her voice.

"Welcome to the dry lands. My name is Dr. Reena Sarkis and we have been expecting you."

Reena had a Mediterranean beauty to her that took Roland's breath away, her silky tan complexion didn't need any make up.

She smelled faintly of perfume, charcoal and suntan lotion. Her curly brown locks danced and played with her shoulders when she moved and framed her expressive olive colored eyes that seemed to hold a secret or a mystery waiting to be discovered. She had an exquisite Roman nose, but always wore a sardonic half grin on her face that made it seem you were the butt of a joke that you weren't a part of.

Roland wasn't bad looking himself, his sun kissed Nubian's skin was a rich dark brown like nappa leather. He looked rugged but not muscular. He didn't crop his hair close to his head, instead he styled his hair in dense corkscrew coils that seemed to fit the strong features of his face perfectly. His eyes were lighter than caramel, but with the same golden tone. It was apparent that Roland didn't keep up with the latest fashion trends but with his looks it didn't really matter.

Dr. Misthos nodded and shook hands with the woman once more while feeling her tight grip. "I was of the impression that I was brought here to… "

"To transcribe some ancient text", Reena completed his sentence for him. "You are indeed right Dr. Misthos."

Roland didn't look pleased and he looked back at his camel while trying to figure out what Reena was thinking; most people couldn't believe he was black. He didn't sugar coat it. He hated the term African American. The assumption that everyone with dark skin origin was from Africa was ridiculous. If people studied their history, they would know most of the population came from Africa before the great migration. Nevertheless, Roland always found himself in a position where he had to prove himself and even then, sometimes he still felt the racist hatred boiling just below the surface of their words. Right now, he was focusing his thoughts on the lack of information provided when he had picked up the project. "Nobody informed me about the need to travel through the hot sands and sun for seven days," he fumed.

He was about to go on a rant, but Reena wasn't having any of it.

"You assumed wrong Dr. Misthos and you know what they say about assumptions," she chuckled softly. "Also, the scrolls are too delicate for us to try and move without damaging them."

Dr. Misthos still saw no reason why he couldn't have been informed before he began his journey. He would have prepared himself better. Instead of suffering he had endured. The wind blowing hot sand in his face, running out of water, and the Egyptian carpet vipers he encountered on no less than three occasions. He was lucky to have even made it to his destination, on more than one occasion he thought about turning around and going back home.

"We are trying to make copies using time-lapse cameras. We know one of the scrolls is in Egyptian hieroglyphics but some of the characters have never been seen before. The other is a rare form of malhip. This third scroll has a text we have never seen before."

"Malhip you say? That's really interesting," Roland said. "Have you been able to translate the first two scrolls?"

Reena laughed. "Let me answer you by saying if we translated them correctly, then I might have to take up religion again."

The doctor had a bewildered look on his face indicating he didn't get the joke.

"There is much to discuss. Of course, you must be tired. Please allow me to drive you back to camp. There you can enjoy a cool bath and some food. I will send someone back to bring the camels the rest of the way. Come."

Roland and Reena got into the jeep and sped off. The loud noise from the engine and the sound of the wind in his ears made it hard to hear.

"You can call me Roland," the doctor informed Reena.

He wasn't sure if the lady had heard him, but he had made his point. Now that he was free of the camel, Roland realized that he did indeed need a bath and a change of clothes, the camel wasn't the only thing that smelled. A bit embarrassed, he edged away from Reena in the hopes that his foul odor didn't offend her.

———————

Roland had been provided for as Reena had assured him. The camp wasn't as bad as he had thought it would be and it wasn't long before he had his belongings and was happy to bathe and wash the desert sand, dust and sweat than clung to him like and old lover off his body. When he went back into his tent, Arabic bread, a bowl of kushari, a piece of basbousa and a cold beer were laid out on a table for him. Roland didn't care much for beer, but it was cold and that's all that mattered. He devoured the meal quickly and drank the beer. He knew he might regret drinking the beer, but he would deal with the consequences later.

The afternoon sun had slowly begun to wane in its effect and strength as the evening approached. He was provided ample time to recuperate from his journey before someone came to the front of his tent to call him out. It was Reena.

"Be ready in twenty minutes," Reena spoke before heading out.

He took the time to rest his head and close his eyes for a moment, he must have dosed off because Reena was calling his name from outside his tent. He got up and left the tent.

He and Reena walked side by side, while those in the camp stood around talking or engaged in the business of the camp. Most of these people seemed to be locals who brought in supplies, stayed the night then left a day or two later. They paid little attention to them as they passed. They finally came before a large tent; bigger than his surprisingly because he had thought he got the biggest by the observations he made.

Roland was about to step in when Reena stopped him momentarily with her hand. "Prepare to have your mind blown," she chuckled.

Roland didn't really understand what she was talking about but managed to let off a weak smile. He noticed upon walking into the sizable tent that there were five huge wood crates piled in the right corner, while a large folding table was in the center of the space. There was just one person in the room, and the man looked engrossed in whatever he was doing.

On the table he noticed there was a medium sized gas lantern and by its side, there were numerous drawings that caught his eye from afar. The work surface also had five chairs arranged around it and in one of the chairs was the man sitting in it and focused on his work. Not even their entrance had made him budge from his spot and it showed just how dedicated he was to what he was

21

doing.

His action piqued Roland's interest as they drew close. He looked up startled upon seeing Reena but stopped what he was working on.

"All of this for a couple of rare scrolls?" Roland exclaimed.

"Dr. Misthos, this is Ralph Ellman. He's one of our researchers not to mention a talented artist. I'm always telling Ralph he got into the wrong profession," Reena said.

Roland nodded, walked over to Ralph and shook the man's hand.

Ralph's blonde corn colored hair was cropped, and it showed off the strong symmetry of his face. The guy had a thin sculptured body that immediately made me think he was a runner. He didn't have an ounce of body fat on him. He looked more like a Hollywood actor than a studious researcher. Moisture beaded across his forehead here in the desert heat, but he didn't sweat like us mere mortals, he glistened.

Ralph laughed a little. "Well it was either this or starve on the streets in Rome as an inspiring artist. I'm guessing you can tell which I picked," he laughed some more. "I've finished drawing the outer hallway."

Roland walked over to admire the drawings and the entire artwork on the table.

"What hallway? What are you talking about?" he inquired.

Roland took another look at the artworks fervently. He took his time on the drawings, committing every inch and corner to his mind. "What am I looking at?" he pointed to a section of the

22

drawing.

Reena bent over to look at it. "That is the Temple of Goulaumx."

It looked beautiful and Roland ran his hand over the image once more.

"It looks fantastic. Where exactly is it?" Roland inquired.

Reena made a gesture pointing downwards to the earth. "About sixty feet below us I believe. We're standing right on it."

Roland looked in awe. He opened his mouth and widened his eyes. "Are you telling me you just found this thing?"

Reena nodded. "It was within this structure that we found the scrolls."

 "I carbon dated the scrolls to be written ninety years before the birth of Christ," Ralph responded. Roland nodded and drew a chair close to him and sat down. "And the structure?"

"The structure is dated to be built 10,000 years earlier," Reena replied.

"Who else knows about this?" Roland asked.

"Besides the three of us, there is Susan Lee our medical doctor and Zachary Ganz. He's the one who found this place. Paradise in the middle of a desert."

 "That's an interesting way to put it... paradise," an unfamiliar voice in the room spoke.

A tall looking man with a faint limp approached Reena and Roland before standing before them. Reena did the necessary introduction. It was her task for the day after all.

"Dr. Roland Misthos this is Zachary Ganz," said Reena.

Roland eyed the man interestingly before shaking his hand.

Zachary was a giant of a man, his head almost touched the top of the tent they were standing in. His face was mostly obscured by lots of soft black hair and he maintained a perfectly groomed moustache and beard. If he had been wearing a toga the man could have been mistaken for Zeus the god and ruler of the Olympians. His eyes were blue and pale like the sky in the early morning. He wore a smirk on his lips as if he had just stolen the last chocolate chip cookie out of the jar but forgot to wipe away the evidence off his face.

"This is the man to confirm our fears I believe?" Zachary Ganz smiled. "It is a pleasure to meet you. Your reputation precedes you, my friend."

Roland had heard just one word in the entire sentence. "Fears? What fears are those?" he was forced to ask.

Reena and the other two men shared a brief look with one another. They knew something he didn't know, and he was the ignorant one in their midst obviously.

"We need to confirm if the third scroll matches the other two," Reena answered the question.

"Were you able to copy the two scrolls?" Zachary turned to Ralph.

Ralph nodded. "I finished the second one this morning", he replied before walking to where he kept them and handed the two scrolls he had copied from the original to Roland.

Roland collected the scrolls from the man carefully like he was handling the original scrolls, before walking over to the table to begin looking at them. He took his time while the others simply left him be. The things he was staring at were fascinating, and he could barely pay them any attention. Zachary approached him from behind before stopping just a few feet from Roland.

The man cleared his throat and held his hands behind his back. "I first got a glimpse of your work in an article in Kenya in the National Geographic two years ago," the man recalled to memory. "It was inspired."

Roland recalled the particular work he was talking about. It was his insights on Mayan glyphic interpretation.

"It was brilliant and also one of the reasons I sent for you since you're named as one of the top linguist in the world," Zachary continued.

Roland smiled wildly. He was being flattered and it was disturbing. He shifted in his chair uncomfortably before turning around to look at the man.

"You flatter me too much sir," Roland managed not to smile. "At best, I'm a pretty good interpreter with a cunning fetish for understanding dead languages."

Zachary knew what he was talking about. He had carried out his research on Roland enough to respect the man who could speak sixty-seven languages had an unrivaled a coherent understanding of 105 writings.

"You are a unique individual Dr. Misthos," Zachary said.

Zachary was simply in awe of the man before him whether he accepted it or not. Roland continued to study the drawings and its content. His synesthesia started to kick in. It was still hard to believe that everyone did not experience graphemes. Roland remembered being surprised when he described written Spanish as having a translucent overlay of redness to it. It was something he kind of sensed more than saw, he realized he would need more time to go through everything.

"Can I take the drawings back to my tent to study them?" he looked up at Zachary to ask.

Zachary nodded his head and agreed. "By all means, go ahead. They were drawn and drafted for you," he urged Roland.

Roland packed up and began preparing to leave when Zachary called him back.

"We will be going to the temple and I'd be honored if you were to accompany us," the man walked over with a hopeful face.

"Nothing would give me greater pleasure," Roland smiled.

He felt like a child on Christmas Eve and Zachary could see it on his face. He took one more look at the drawings in his hand heading out the tent in slow walk. Zachary watched the man walk away before sighing to himself.

"I wish I shared your sentiments," he muttered underneath his breath to himself.

Roland walked back to his tent his mind spinning with thoughts. He walked into his tent, dragged the table provided to him from the corner of the space to the center of the tent. He settled into the chair and piled up some reference books he might need and helped himself to a lantern.

He began work immediately. He began flipping through the pages of a reference book to find what he was seeking. He took out a black marble notebook and began scribbling his findings. He had a long night ahead of him to make findings and come to some reasonable conclusions, the night wasn't going to be enough.

CHAPTER FIVE

Roland loved physically writing things down, it helped him with his thought process. There was something about working out thoughts and problems down on paper.

It wasn't the same typing on a computer or using a tablet, Roland loved the smell of the paper and the feel of the pen or pencil in his hand. It put him on another level.

Just like the moment he was in now. His hand couldn't keep up with his thoughts, this is the most excited he has been about anything in a long while. As a child, Roland never believed in Santa Claus, but this must be the feeling a child has on Christmas Eve right before he must go to bed. For the first time in a long while, Roland didn't know what to expect.

He had transcribed the other scrolls rather quickly, all of them in different languages but they told the same story. Roland studied the drawing of the scroll, his synesthesia kicked in and he nearly fainted. That's never happened to him before.

When the language came alive in his mind he was assaulted with so many colors and smells that it made his head spin. Normally the way his synesthesia worked is that he associated certain letters with certain colors and a different language might take on a certain hue of color along with a certain smell.

The Spanish language always took on a red hue in his vision accompanied by the smell of smoked paprika. A different dialect, like the Spanish spoken in Puerto Rico has a deep red color that his mind associated with it, unlike Spain which looked more magenta in color with the slight smell of cumin.

This strange language however had him seeing waves of color and the odors he smelled kept changing. At first, he smelled frankincense, then lavender, suddenly cloves assaulted his nostrils.

Roland jumped out of his chair and barely made it out of the tent before he retched in the desert sand.

After a long moment outside, Roland walked back in to the tent and found a canteen of water next to his cot. He took a long drink to get the bitter taste out of his mouth.

What just happened? Roland thought to himself. This new language seems to be alive. He knew it didn't make sense but that was the only way he could describe it.

He sat on his cot for a moment and thought about how he could puzzle out this particular dilemma. An idea struck him, and he walked over to the table careful not to look at the scroll, he grabbed one of his marble notebooks and covered up a portion of the scroll only leaving only a small part of the text visible.

After a moment of hesitation, he looked at the scroll. Roland sighed in relief, his idea worked. Although still unsettling, it was much easier to look at the scroll just a small section at a time, instead of all at once.

The other scroll the one with the new languages was a mystery. It was something completely new. Comparing it with the scrolls will take some time but he had an idea that might work.

This was completely new, and it was wonderful. Roland wrote ideas and theories in his notebook well into the night. Looking up the history of the people indigenous to this area in the hope of linking something, anything, sometime late into the night or early in to the morning pending on how you looked at it, Roland finally stopped working and went to sleep.

CHAPTER SIX

The first night in the camp wasn't the best, the translation didn't go as smoothly as he had hoped. The day had been hot, but the cold in the desert at night was worse than Roland had imagined.

To make things worse, the little hours of sleep he had hoped to gain had been interrupted by the occasional clinking and clanking of objects in the tent and the howling of night creatures he couldn't identify. He felt drugged by morning and had bags underneath his eyes, which was noticeable for anyone willing to take note. His experience so far hadn't been bad or entirely comfortable, but he wasn't there for the comfort.

He was there to work and that was all that mattered, and he had to meet with the others at the temple entrance.

The opening to the temple looked like a giant hole in the sand. The only thing that marked the opening was a blue flag. Susan Lee, Ralph Ellman, Reena Sarkis and Zachary Ganz stood outside of the opening drinking coffee.

Susan stood there deep in thought. For a long time, she said nothing, she stared into her coffee as if her gaze could bring the dark liquid back to a hot steaming boil, as if she could dump all were worries and fears in to its murky depths. Susan had a classic chic European look to her, the kind of woman other women hated because it took her no effort at all to look beautiful. She was quite easy to admire; her short pixie cut blond hair complimented her face. She had a long slender figure showing no curves to her body at all but still came off as being sexy even in the tee shirt and jeans she wore now.

31

Susan hadn't taken a sip from stainless steel mug in about five minutes and Ralph had taken note.

"Something bothering you Susan?" he called out to her.

They stopped taking sips from their mugs to look at her.

"I'm thinking we should be more careful today," she spoke with a hint of worry in her voice.

"You worry too much Susan. You should loosen up a little," Zachary encouraged her.

"The nearest hospital is over forty miles away. We were lucky the last time. The only reason why Ralph didn't die is because I happened to have had the right serum for that snake bite. If I didn't do my homework we- ," Susan pleaded.

"It is why I wanted you to come on this trip. I wouldn't feel safe if you weren't by my side. We all feel safer in your presence."

Susan remained bullish. She sighed and crossed her arms over her chest.

"When I asked to walk with sand underneath my feet, you know I had a rather different image in mind than this right?" she smiled at Zachary.

Zachary approached her with his arms spread apart. He wrapped them around her slowly and intimately before holding her by her waist. He pressed his lips on to hers and they made up immediately. It was their thing to give each other a hard time only to make things straight a moment later.

"If it's any consolation, I'm glad you're here too," Ralph reminded her.

Susan blushed and winked at him before taking a sip from her mug once again. Zachary drained his own cup of coffee and tossed the stainless-steel mug into an empty crate on the ground. Reena on the other hand continued to stare into her mug as though she waited for something to happen. The mug remained full and barely touched even thought she had raised it to her lips a few times.

Ralph poured the remaining coffee in his mug into the sand, while watching it get absorbed immediately. They all turned their attention to Roland who had an eager look on his face. As he approached the opening to the temple.

He had the drawings rolled up neatly and carefully underneath his arm while holding a black marble notebook in his left hand.

"Good morning guys. It is good to see you," Roland greeted.

"Good morning doctor, I hope you had a good night rest?" Zachary walked forward.

Roland shook his head. "How does one sleep when you have made the discovery of a lifetime? I spent most of the night and early morning had to transcribing the text."

They looked at him like he had done something strange. The work was extensive and the fact he was claiming he had done it all through the night was crazy. Roland read from a note book where he kept his notes. He had transcribed exactly what was written so parts of the translation read like broken English. Certain phrases didn't have a direct translation. Roland did his best to fill in the gaps.

"The first couple of pages is a history. A myth really, of a time when god like beings walked the earth. They ruled over fantastic creatures of nature as well as the men of the earth," he explained.

They looked at him in awe and with confusion lining their faces.

"They ruled over these fantastic creatures of nature as well as the men of the earth. I assume this refers to regular people like you and I," he whispered interestingly.

"The men and the creatures worshipped these god like beings for their life spans out lasted their own. So, it came past that the gods were divided between the dark and the light and a great war broke out throughout the lands everywhere. These god like beings were hunted as minions of evil, they became fewer and fewer, and went into hiding deep within the earth and the seas and in special places in the world that could not be seen. Some will hide among us pretending to be us until the time comes when we will live as one in harmony."

They gasped and fell silent.

Roland hadn't realized just how stunned they were.

"Is everything alright?" Roland inquired.

Zachary looked calmer than the others though. "How much of a climber are you doctor? We need to go into the temple."

Roland heard the word "climb" and looked stricken with shock.

"The opening to the temple is an eighty-foot drop and having another tragic accident resulting in another man's death wouldn't be acceptable," Reena recounted in discomforting tone.

"Be careful of the vipers and other creatures down there too," Susan warned.

Roland gulped down hard and thought about all they had just told him.

Roland had never done any kind of rock climbing in his life, he was both scared and excited. Reena outfitted him with the gear he would need to make the journey.

She put the climbing harness on him and adjusted it until it felt comfortable to him, placed the head lamp on his head and went over the climbing ropes, carabiners, pully and belay device and discussed how to use them properly.

One by one the team of people lower themselves into the hole. Roland is second to last with Reena bringing up the rear. Being surrounded completely in darkness like this was otherworldly and unearthly. It was easy to lose track of time. The group had only been in the darkness for ten minutes, but Roland's mind began to wander as he wondered about different things.

Roland knew what sensory deprivation was but knowing something and actually experiencing it are two completely different things.

Sensory deprivation was simply the removal or reduction of stimuli from one of the five senses. For Roland it was his sight. Moments after the group entered the temple, the temperature dropped at least ten degrees.

Roland was confused at first when the group had all donned head lamps but after descending about twenty feet it became clear. The light from the entrance above almost disappeared in the darkness. Soon the only thing Roland could see were the other head lamps floating above and below him.

Roland recalled a study that a friend of his did at Harvard, it was a study to test the effect sensory deprivation had on the brain.

Some of the test subjects saw faces that were not actually there. Others reported losing all sense of reality or even sensing the presence of something dark and not of this world.

Roland wondered to himself why everyone was moving in such a straight line. Floating here in zero gravity among the stars in space was so much fun. Maybe he should float over to Reena.

"Roland... Roland", a distant voice called out to him.

The unseen voice called out to him again, startling him and making the man fidget on his lifeline as he looked around in wonder of who it was or could be. The voice sounded familiar, almost like an old friend calling out to a loved one. He continued to turn his head and with it the headlamp in a manner that made Zachary call out to Roland again. A hint of urgency tinged his voice as he took note of the man's discomfort.

"Don't stop doctor," the Zachary warned. "Don't think about getting to the bottom! It will come soon enough! Remember one hand under the other! Take your time. You're doing absolutely fabulous for a beginner," he affirmed.

Roland was barely listening to the man above him. He had almost let go of his lifeline. His heart pounded in fear as his mind came back to reality.

Roland managed to pull himself out of the dark place his mind was in and slowly came back to reality. With sweat still running down his face, he smiled; "This is actually incredible! I feel like I'm in space!"

It wasn't a lie, moments ago he truly believed he was in outer space floating in zero gravity. If he had let the fantasy take over, it could of cost them all dearly.

Zachary as if he had read Roland's thoughts cautioned the man once again, "Just remember doc that once you let go of the rope for any reason, you will drop like a lead weight and possibly drag us down with you."

If Zachary only knew just how close they had come to making his statement a reality. The thought made Roland shutter. He heeded the man's warning and continued at a steady pace. Suddenly below him there was an explosion of light and Roland was suddenly aware that they were in a large chamber and only about twenty feet from touching the ground. The entire experience only took about twenty minutes, but it had felt like hours.

Thump! Thump! Thump!

Their shoes hammered the ground intermittently with the mixed sounds of sighs and relief from everyone.

The room was a large, circular space no less than fifty feet in diameter and to his right, from where he stood was a visible corridor. He gazed towards the corridor while the others finished packing their gear in place. An altar stood in the center of the room, bringing his focus to it. He approached the fascinating looking object with curiosity.

Mounds surrounded the altar, they were probably used for seating. It was as if someone had thrown a pebble into a clear, still lake, just as the ripples formed, something froze the lake in place, thereby locking them in a state of stillness with the ripples in view as well as the pebble which had created them.

On the dome of the altar, was an intricately detailed painting of angels, demons and beasts as well as other creatures of fantasy tossed into the mix.

"This is remarkable," Roland attested, falling to his knees in the process.

He was completely mesmerized by what he saw before him.

Ralph chuckled briefly, "I had the same reaction when I first saw it too."

Roland couldn't take his eyes off the painting. "My God!"

Ralph approached the mesmerized man where he remained on his knees. He took a good look at the painting and felt himself relive the moment he had first seen it over again. The majestic work of art was truly a depiction of the beauty in God's work and his wonders. They shared the sight for a brief second.

"Ten thousand years before the birth of Christ! Nothing found during this era matches this find. It makes the Renaissance look like a child's party. Before the rise and fall of the Roman empire. Before the Greeks and the Incas," Ralph stated passionately.

Roland turned back to look at the paintings. His eyes widened, and his lips curled disbelief. "How is this possible?" he thought to himself.

Reena joined Roland and Ralph. "Now you understand Dr. Misthos. Come let me show you where the tomb and the original scrolls were found."

CHAPTER SEVEN

Reena led Roland the tomb chamber also with a dome shaped ceiling, the floor was made of smooth black marble. How and where did these people get black marble was beyond Roland's comprehension.

Nothing in this chamber should be here or even exist during the time that Zachary and his team claim this structure was created. Roland could not believe his eyes, the first chamber left him dumbfounded this chamber left him speechless.

In the center of the room on display were three crystal coffins as clear as glass. The bodies of the dead were completely intact and looked ageless.

It must have been a trick of the light because at one point, Roland swore he saw one of the bodies breathing as if asleep.

The three coffins were carefully placed in the center of the chamber with their heads facing each other in an arrangement mirroring a three-point star. He walked towards the white crystal encased sarcophagi, each of the vessels had a black marble cylinder container that was placed on the seamless lid of each casket. Inside each of the cylinders was a scroll.

Of the three bodies, two were men and the third, a woman. They all looked like they were in their forties. One of the men had long black and white hair and around his forehead was a gold headband.

Roland was fascinated and exchanged a quick glance with Reena who waited for the doctor to do his thing.

"How is this even possible?" he marveled.

He examined the headband to see a round shaped ruby placed in the center of it, his skin was pale yellow in complexion. Even with the eyes closed Roland guessed the man was of Asian descent. Roland took a good look at the body, carving every single feature into his mind, before moving over to the second male who had a grey moustache and beard. The second man had an identical headband like his counterpart except his skin complexion was that of a light-colored coffee and might be European. The lady on the other hand had long radiant copper colored red hair extending all the way to her waist and with an almond complexion. Her origins were impossible to place.

He turned to Reena, "These bodies are in perfect condition. How on earth is that possible?"

Reena got closer to the coffins, "The coffins must be void of air."

"I would have thought this sort of technique wasn't discovered until centuries after this period?" Roland noted.

Evidently, he was wrong.

He continued to marvel at the wonders before him. He gushed and grinned while even trying to touch the coffin before deciding against it.

"Do you want to know the most disturbing and puzzling part of it all?" Reena asserted.

 "There are no lids on the coffins. There are no seams. We don't have a clue as to how they got in there," she explained.

"Are you joking?" Roland exclaimed in bewilderment as he brushed the hair out of his face.

He walked over to inspect the coffins closely again. To his utmost surprise and disbelief, she was right about the lidless coffins and the mysteries behind them. He took his time with the coffins before Reena let out a soft cough intended to gain his attention.

"I hate to sound like a pushy bitch Dr. Misthos, but it is who I am, and I need to know if you deciphered the third scroll yet," she grinned.

He took time away from the coffins to speak with her.

"The first two scrolls I have translated basically say the same thing. The story of these god like beings walking the earth, disappearing and then someday returning. If I assume the third scroll says the same thing I might be able to figure out a basic alphabet. But if it is the same what's the point of decoding it? I mean of course it's interesting to me. The discovery of a new language is fascinating and fantastic but why are you pushing me? What interest is it to you?"

Zachary responded instead of Reena, "I can answer that question for you Dr. Misthos, follow me if you please."

Reena turned to Zachary with a sketchy look on her face. "I don't know if he has to know this Zach or if we should tell him at all," she whispered to him.

"What choice do we have?" Zachary stated flatly.

"What are you talking about?" Roland said impatiently as he crossed his arms over his chest.

Zachary and Reena walked out of the chamber they were in and Roland followed them. They ventured into another room which

42

was inconspicuous enough for him not to take note of earlier before Zach pointed to it.

"This Dr. Misthos," he said.

Upon entering the room, Zachary turned on a portable light on the floor. The room burst into visible scenery and with it, the square shape of the room came to view.

There was nothing in it except for a black marble chair. Roland approached the chair, only to notice Reena and Zachary staring at the walls. They seemed rather engrossed by whatever they were looking at, prompting him to do the same in hopes of ascertaining what took their fancy.

He had missed it before; the four walls weren't blank but covered with strange writings that made Roland gasp immediately. "My God! Oh my God!"

Roland's synesthesia kicked in. He quickly closed his eyes and waited to become violently ill like he did in his tent, instead he became aware of the scent of incense, the smell was strong but not unpleasant. Roland gradually opened his eyes and saw waves of rainbow colored ripples dancing and moving across the strange text on the walls. Colors only his mind eye could see. The room also had a low hum in the background, there was no reaction from the others, so Roland guessed he must be the only one hearing it as well.

Zachary sighed and held out his hands towards the walls, "I see you understand now Dr. Misthos, as this is the first of the eight identical rooms and I need to know what the strange writings on the walls say."

The question was definitely there for him to look at. Roland didn't need anyone asking it or spelling the words out. He already asked himself if he was ready for where the journey would lead him.

He saw things no one else could see but him. He had to know as much as they needed to know.

Zachary spoiled the moment slightly by eventually asking, "What do you think Dr. Misthos? Are you up for the challenge of your life?"

Roland didn't turn to look at him immediately.

"I need to return to the surface to do some research first," he responded without looking away from the markings in strange tongue on the wall. A language that was lost to time.

Reena and Zachary shared a brief look with one another before she stepped forward. She ran her hand across the wall touching it lightly. "This could become a marvelous discovery for us all."

Roland didn't doubt it.

"It could tell us more about the universe, provide cures to persistent diseases and possibly the long-forgotten secret to immortality," she continued in full throttle of excitement.

Reena momentarily looked away from the wall. Zachary didn't share the same look of excitement on his face. He usually was more passionate about finding new things, especially those of alien origin like the one they stood before.

Zachary sighed, cleared his throat and replied, "My fear is it could be a beginning to an end. A type of revelations like in the bible. To put it simply the end of everything."

He was making some sense, but Roland cut in to give another angle to his thoughts, "Or maybe the continuation of something started long ago. It could be the continuation of life."

He didn't disbelieve in what worried Zachary, but he hoped and prayed within for something different too. They all were worried about their findings now. They all were troubled by what might come of things and the room fell silent immediately.

CHAPTER EIGHT

A vast jungle city existed where no city should exist, yet it did. This was the first time in the history of the world that a city was discovered miles below the earth. The only thing to come close was the underground city of Derinkuyu in Turkey.

That city is approximately two hundred feet below ground and was big enough to have around twenty thousand people living and working together. This however in every sense of the word was impossible, unimaginable and inconceivable.

Michael and Keith were miles below the earth, the pressure and heat form the earth's core should have killed them according to modern science. The scientific method didn't even exist here. There is blue sky above and a sun. Trees and animals that have never been seen by human eyes before, well at least human eyes from the world where Michael and Keith come from, there is a race of people down here speaking a language the two scientists had never heard before. A civilization in a place of dreams and fantasy, the air is heavy with the scent of earth and the aroma filled Keith's senses as his thoughts echoed in his head.

"If I hadn't seen it with my own eyes I would have not believed it. This place has existed for God know how long. We have been here for over five months and every day something amazes me. Who would ever believe that this place has its own separate sun apart of our own. I don't understand it. A city with people underneath the earth. We have been able to communicate with the people somewhat through hand signals and body movement. Michael, I believe is slowly beginning to understand their strange language. It sounds like a child's dream. It's like magic. That was something

I never believed in, until now."

They were in the "Devils Fork" now, and it was mesmerizing to be in.

Keith was an impatient man with an optimistic outlook on life. It was his optimism that convinced Michael that getting into the Fork was even possible. He was a little shorter than average with a medium solid build, a round face and a receding hazel-brown hairline that gave him a Nicolas Cage vibe, like the actor he was good looking, but you couldn't really put a finger on why, his shadowed blue eyes, dark eyebrows along with his hawk nose and thin lips completed the effect. He didn't look like a researcher or a doctor in his perfectly tailored casual clothing.

Michael on the other hand was very tall with a muscular build. With his shirt partially open you could see the striated muscles beneath the skin and his skeletal frame. He was clearly a bit underweight and cause for every Italian mother with in a five-mile radius to chase him around with a plate of food begging him to eat something. His features were striking, his hair was thin, dark brown and brushed backward forming perfect straight lines to the back of his neck. Michael's long face and high cheekbones in combination with his amber, sunken eyes gave him an air of nobility and made him look older than he was. There was a portrayal of intelligence in the way that he spoke and gestured that the average person would find intimidating.

The two men walk down a dirt path that has been covered with gravel, most likely to keep the vegetation from growing it's amazing how inventive this people are. The people of this world walk and talk among themselves in a language Keith and Michael have never heard before. Keith's thoughts echo in his head.

"Their language is magical... this place is magical, and it feels like living in a child's dream. I never would have believed it unless I saw it for myself. I have seen it and it is remarkable."

Keith turns to Michael.

"The soil samples are rich. The most fertile ever found. Which will probably explain why everything grows so fast and rich here."

Michael stopped to share his thoughts with his friend. "Or maybe unlike us, they give a damn about where they live and decide not to pollute, contaminate the land, but keep it clean at all times," he interjected.

Keith shook his head at his colleague. "I'm sorry, but how many times do I have to say it to you Mike? It was just a candy wrapper!"

"Yes Keith, it was just a candy wrapper," Michael replied in sarcasm.

"A candy wrapper from our world, which we know nothing about how it would come to affect their environment," Michael argued.

They had agreed to burn everything they brought with them from their own world once they were done making use of them. Michael had just gotten through speaking when a child ran over and began to tug at his arm. He looked at the little being and smiled. He recognized the child to be Danatu.

The boy was small but had thoughtful dark eyes full of intelligence beyond his years. His smile brought with it a friendliness that instantly made you feel happy. He had become the village liaison often dragging the two men all over, but Michael was the only one who truly understood him.

"Botami! Botami ka firatu!" Danatu the child yelled while tugging at his arm.

Keith looked lost, "What is he talking about?"

"He wants me to come with him…", Michael replied, while looking a little bit puzzled.

Keith nodded and urged him on. "I will meet you in the village later. You should go with the boy."

"Thanks, I will see you in about two hours," Michael spoke over his shoulder while allowing the boy to lead him away.

Keith walked in the opposite direction; down the road they were initially headed. He had peace to some extent at last, but wondered what Michael was being summoned for. He would find out later though. Michael walked south with the boy into the village and they both disappeared into the distance and out of each other's sights.

Michael arrived with the little boy in the village popularly known as the "Village of Matra." It was noon already and the walk had been quite exhaustive. They approached a small stone house.

The house looked like yurt. A yurt is a portable, round tent covered with the skins and felts of animals used by certain tribes in Central Asia. These houses had that similar round designed but seemed to be made of mud and clay. The roof however was the same, constructed of animal skins with a hole at the top to allow light in to the structure.

He turned to Michael and said nothing. Michael guessed they

arrived at their destination.

The boy led Michael in to the small stone house. He had just walked in when he noticed the reason he was summoned. A sick woman whose body continued to shudder vigorously was the reason the boy had come and beckoned him. She was without doubt, really sick, as she was soaked in cold sweat.

The people here don't seem to have any kind of medicine.

What medicine Michael and Keith had with them, they used months ago, on themselves and some of the people in the village, now whenever someone is sick or in disease the people from the village come and gets Michael to help.

Michael was not a medical doctor and most of what he did to ease and help these people he learned from his grandmother. There is a meat in this world that tastes a lot like chicken, although both Michael and Keith have yet to see a chicken in this world he hopes that it is some kind of fowl and not a rat or some other creature that they would rather not eat if it could be helped.

Whatever it was, the people called it megar, he asked for the megar as well as some other vegetables. Over the past month through trial and error Michael had come up with something that tasted like chicken soup.

He had also come up with a healing tea and luckily found willow trees in this world that he could make aspirin from. Not many people know this but making a tea from the willow bark will cure most headaches and relieve minor pain.

So, in a short amount of time, Michael became the local healer, much to the dismay of the village healer. Michael was quick to teach the village doctor everything he knew so it wouldn't upset the hierarchy, the village doctor learned quickly and was still respected, however the villagers still called on Michael every now and then to help. Michael didn't mind. It was nice to be needed. An old man bent over her, appearing to be praying for the sick lady.

Danatu stared at Michael deeply, "Ti au batamu. Gera!"

The old man was thin, tall and bony and his white hair danced around his face as if it had a life of its own, he stood next to the old man, they were the same height which put them eye to eye, His dark brown soulful eyes had such a range of expressions in them that it was hard to tell what the man was thinking. His name was Farama and his voice was mixed with worry.

"Mikel. Ma zi ku detava". He spoke softly.

"Detava, water! I'll bring you water," Michael responded and headed out of the room.

He ran to a nearby well and found an object with which he draws some water into a small pail and brings it over to Farama, the old man.

"Guryti", the old man said in gratitude before collecting the water from Michael.

Michael pulled out some willow's bark from his pocket. He pointed to the bark then pointed to the water and made a drinking motion with his hands.

Understanding, the old man took the water Michael had given him and poured it in to a copper kettle and put the kettle over the fire with the bark inside. It soon came to a boil. The old man then poured the liquid into a clay cup.

Cooling the tea with his own lips, he gently held the water to the woman's lips for her to have a drink from. Michael found a cloth in his backpack, he dipped the cloth in the willow tea, rung it out and placed it on the woman's forehead.

Michael softly called to the man by tapping his shoulder. He pointed to himself and then at the woman which made Farama step backwards and bow gently in the process of doing so.

"We need something to keep her warm," Michael muttered to himself.

He looked around the room to find a blanket, he rushed over to grab it and quickly returned to the woman to wrap it around her shivering body. It took some doing, but the woman eventually stopped shaking and her breath slowly eased into the right rhythm.

Michael watched her get comfortable and heard Farama laugh loudly and joyously behind him. He turned to see the man bowing in respect.

"Oei se tiga mo Zar!" he said while pointing up into the sky for Michael to look in the direction of his hand.

Michael looked up not quite understanding what Farama meant. Farama lifted his hand and pointed up again before speaking.

"Zar!" he spoke aloud.

Michael smiled and looked up again to be sure he was seeing things as he should. He still didn't seem to be getting the point intended and Farama approached him to take Michael by the arm and led him outside of the small stone house. Together, they walked to the center of the village without saying a word to each other. Michael was confused without doubt but kept on smiling in hopes he would come to understand what the man wanted pretty soon.

Learning their ways and their language didn't come easy and it included several moments like the one he was now involved in. While they walked past people, the villagers gently bowed their heads in respect to the two men.

They made their way to the biggest structure in the entire village.

Michael recognized the building. It was one of the first things he saw upon arriving there. They walked towards the pyramid that reminded Michael of the Inca civilization. The beautiful temple adorned with crystal and gold was breathtaking to his sight as he looked around. The old man led him into the structure.

In the middle of the room they walked into was a crystal that looked like it was floating. It was suspended in mid-air and the crystal was shaped like a three-dimensional Christmas tree star. The crystal star glowed brightly and in pale blue. In the room were five women in white dresses, standing underneath the crystal and singing beautifully in melodious tone unlike anything he had heard before. Michael was in awe and wonder of their voices when Farama pulled him away from where he stood.

They journeyed away from the room and into another to his right. The room was different in shape and unlike any he had seen either. The dome-shaped room with a fantastic display of artworks painted all over it attracted the man immediately. He could literarily feel his entire essence and soul leave him to enjoy the beauty of the paintings and art works on the wall. He would have thought he was in another world had he been blindfolded before stepping into the room.

It was by far the most beautiful discovery he had come to see in his life since he was born and since he arrived in the new world. Farama points to painted scene where a winged man flies to the sick person and takes the sick person away this caption is followed by a picture of this bird man healing the sick and bringing the sick back healthy and happy. Farama points to the winged creature.

"What is all this?" Michael asked, knowing he still couldn't figure out what the old man was trying to show him.

Farama pointed at the winged creature and spoke, "Zar!"

Michael mirrored his action and did the same, "Zar!"

Farama tenderly bowed his head towards Michael.

Michael hurriedly dug his hand into his pocket to take out his note-pad and scribbled down the word "Zar" and wrote "God" next to it, indicating what he perceived the meaning to be. The book contained other strange words he had scribbled with their meaning in English written by their side. It was his way of keeping tabs on new words and further understanding their language.

Slowly and carefully, he wrapped a rubber band around the note-pad before sticking back into his pocket from where he had taken it out earlier. Michael turned his attention back to Farama, the old man looking at him, gently wiped his hand across his own eyes.

He accompanied the motion with the word "Karupa!"

Michael repeated the words, "Karupa. Karupa. Ka", and he bowed gently before taking his leave.

CHAPTER NINE

Keith is digging in the dirt, he is collecting soil samples for later testing. He has never seen soil like this, in the real world, or at least the world Keith is accustomed to, sampling and analyzing the soil will give you physical and chemical information like if the soil has an excess in salts or a high or low potential hydrogen level otherwise known as pH when you are testing the acidity of the soil, along with looking at the soil texture and nutrient levels.

This is by far the richest soil he has ever seen, of course he would have to test it in a lab to be sure, but it seemed to have a good balance of sand, clay and silt.

The soil was also like volcanic soil because it was dark and rich. It had a fresh, pleasant clean earthy odor.

One of the villagers working with Keith pulled a giant worm out of the ground that was at least fifteen feet in length and looked to be about thirty pounds. The villager held up the worm for Keith to see. Keith didn't see the worm until he caught the movement out from the corner of his eye.

Keith jumped back startled. "Holy shit! Will you look at the size of that thing!"

He looked around and saw they didn't understand a word of what he had said, prompting him to find another way to make his point known to them.

With his hand gesticulating to show the length, he spoke again, "Big fucking worm!"

Huiahd, the villager with the worm responded, "Punami!"

Keith didn't understand his word but nodded. "Well, I don't think that sucker will fit into the sample jar, so you can just let it go."

His words bore no meaning to them still and they continued to stare at him. The villagers waited for him to gesticulate once more; it was the means by which they understood or at least managed to act like they understood anything he was saying to them.

He shook his head and sighed.

"Free! The worm can go free!" he gesticulated as best as he could.

They looked at him, before bursting into laughter. A familiar voice behind him. Told the villagers what they needed to know.

"Sabtoa Hi Zeda", Michael said to the villager with the worm.

The villagers smiled at one another while bowing towards Michael. The one with the worm gently laid it to the ground and chopped it into three with his blade. Keith and Michael watched on as he tossed one of the pieces of worm into his mouth, followed by an endless chewing.

Keith shrieked immediately upon seeing the act, "Oh Christ!"

Michael didn't look at all fazed. He simply laughed at Keith and his inability to truly comprehend their ways. His laughter spurred on the other villagers.

"I believe it tastes just like chicken," Michael informed his ignorant and irritated friend.

Keith obviously thought otherwise but was in no mood to argue. "Where have you been?" he inquired.

Michael pointed over his shoulder without looking back into the distance. "I've been with the old man all day."

"What did he want?" Keith continued. "You guys were gone for awfully long time."

Michael explained how the little boy Danatu had called on him to come tend to the sick lady whom he had realized later, was his mother.

Keith cut him short.

"Wait a minute… hold on buddy", he spoke. "What do you mean sick?"

"Yeah, sick, as in she had the shakes and fever but…"

Keith's face grew rather sour with a frown.

"Are you out of your bloody mind? You have a conniption about a candy bar wrapper but infecting us with God knows what is okay?" Keith vented.

Michael chuckled at the man's drama, "It was just a fever Keith, calm down."

His worries were valid though. They were in a strange place where they had hoped falling sick or anything of such wasn't even possible. Everything had been running smoothly since they arrived, the last thing the needed was to become sick themselves.

He hadn't really thought it through when he saw the sick lady earlier. His instincts to help her had kicked in and blurred out the cautious side he should have listened to. As much as Keith was being overly paranoid, he still should have been more careful.

"Trust me, it is just a fever," he said again. "She just had a fever and I stepped in to help."

Keith snorted rudely, "You hope it is a fever! What are you now, a doctor?"

Michael shook his head.

"You are a doctor in the fields of anthropology and seismology and I am a research scientist which doesn't allow us the effrontery to do as we please with diseases."

They shared a brief silence between them, staring at the villagers who looked on in confusion as the sun continued to beat down upon them.

"Has it even occurred to you that we could die down here?" Keith resumed. "We could fucking die, if you contracted anything deadly in this place."

Michael had had enough of it already; "We could die at any time here Keith... don't you think I see that?"

Michael walked away a couple of feet from Keith with his back turned and stood by a tree with his head touching its trunk.

Keith approached his colleague and friend with a somber heart and mood. He gently reached out and laid his hand on the man's shoulder.

"I'm sorry I blew up at you like that," he apologized. "We both have been under a lot of pressure lately in the past weeks and it has gotten to me."

Michael made no move to look at the apologetic man behind him. He had a lot running through his mind.

"Mike. I'm sorry I blew up at you like that. We both have been under a lot of pressure the past couple of weeks. I've known you for twenty-five years. Even when we were kids, you always took things as they came. I'm overwhelmed to the extreme. Christ, I just saw someone eat part of a fifteen-foot worm!"

Michael couldn't hold a grudge against the apologetic fellow. They shared a quick laugh at his words.

"Not to mention that you're the only one I can talk too. No one else here speaks my language! So, forgive me if I take it out on you buddy."

Michael had heard enough to know the man was sorry. Keith naturally had been known to go overboard with his actions when his emotions ran wild.

"Believe it or not, things get to me too," Michael turned to finally look at his friend. "You may be right about me always leaping before I look, and it isn't a habit I should continue."

Keith's mood lightened. "So, what did the old man say?"

Michael had almost forgotten about the old man and their little trip to the strange rooms.

"Today he showed me their god Zar," Michael explained.

Keith's eyes widened in shock. "He showed you?"

Michael nodded, "After I helped the women, he took me to the pyramid. Keith, I've never see anything like it. It's truly immaculate. The inside of the temple is decked out with crystal and gold. We have been invited to the ceremony tonight."

Keith looked as his friend with some doubt.

"You are kidding about getting invited right? You mean they invited you to their ceremony and you are sure you heard this?" he wanted to be sure. "Does this mean you cracked their language already?"

Michael shook his head, "I must sound like a toddler struggling for words to speak, Farama showed me drawings."

Keith still looked lost. He wanted more information to work with. "Are you talking about stick figures like in a cave?"

"No, these paintings will put Michelangelo to shame. You should come with me tonight and I will show it to you."

Keith sighed and turned around to look at the villagers behind him. He frowned subtly and sighed afterwards, "I will go with you only if you promise they will not eat giant worms."

The two men laughed long and hard.

CHAPTER TEN

Preparations had been made and expectations were high. It seemed like the whole village was assembled around a twenty-foot altar made of wood.

On top of the altar a woman was wrapped in a blanket. The villagers were all on their knees humming. Keith stared on in wonderment and fear.

He didn't know what to expect and prayed to god that this wasn't a human sacrifice like in the Maya culture. The Mayans used to offer nourishment to the gods in the form of blood. If he remembered correctly the most common form of human sacrifice was heart extraction.

A memory of one of the Indiana Jones movies came to him when he pictured it in his mind. Unlike in the movie the heart extraction was most likely influenced by the Aztecs.

Depending on the ritual the heart would be pulled out of the sacrifice just below the left breast while it was still beating then smeared on the likeness of the deity.

Keith shuttered at the thought. The humming from the crowd was hypnotic, it sounded like bees in the hive only deeper. The sound seemed to vibrate his very soul. Keith and Michael walked in to the group and knelt.

"Are we meant to do that too?" Keith raised an eyebrow.

Michael paid him little attention. He didn't hum, but he kept his mind and eyes focused on the lady wrapped in blanket up above.

"It is incredible the entire village is rallying around one of their own in her time of need," Keith said to himself in a whisper.

"Isn't it amazing to see what people will do when they collectively believe in the same thing?" Michael whispered.

Keith looked up at the woman up above, "What happens now?"

"If my instincts and understanding of the drawings I saw are correct, they will call out to their god during the ceremony," Michael enlightened his colleague.

Keith watched on impatiently. The villagers continued to hum and sway in chorus with nothing happening or threatening to happen from what he could see. Keith wanted answers and looked towards Michael expectedly.

"They will light the torch over her head and I believe their god Zar, will descend from the heavens to take her away," Michael pointed while explaining.

Keith exchanged his gaze from Michael to the villagers he looked back and forth between the two and something finally began to happen.

Out of the woods came three men dressed in brown and white feathered cloaks. Each man had a burning torch in hand, and each torch burning brightly radiated in a different color to one another. One torch burned a bright yellow, while the other torch burned an eerie green and the last torch burned a blood red respectively. The men approached the altar walking majestically without looking away from it. Slowly, they began running in circles around the altar.

Michael wondered how they did it. It's funny how people don't even think why a thing does what it does. Wood burning camp fires or torches produce yellow or orange flames because of the salts in the wood.

In his world, Michael would use chemicals to change the color of the flames but did these people have access to those chemicals? To make green flames Michael knew you needed borax. Borax is something that is found in nature, usually in evaporated seasonal lakes.

Borax is most commonly used to wash clothes. He wondered if these people found Borax and used it in the same fashion. A yell from one of the men with the torches brought Michael out of his thoughts and back to the ceremony.

Keith tried to figure out exactly what was going on, but he was permitted no such time, as another man came running out of the woods, bearing a twenty-foot long torch in his hands and that man was none other than Farama.

"Poo Greta Sa cato. Len yea fi Maoti Far grite. Neo Be daowe o harlar, " Farama chanted.

"Che key ta Zar!" the entire crowd with the exception of Michael and Keith chorused after him. It was now apparent ritual was being performed.

"Ya bo feas ven deo. Beltartas I fe solarvi," Farama continued.

"Che key ta Zar!" the crowd chorused again.

Keith was intrigued by what was going on. He wouldn't miss any of it for anything in the world.

"Ge for ha mae Olar! A mei all to ei. Wifeo ila yea sig! Tem aoer kiou! De Gera ai quzo!" Farama yelled louder than ever this time around.

He stretched the torch in his hand over the crowd and the group suddenly fell into a deeper hum than they resonated before. Farama raised the long torch back to an upright position before yelling; "Gei au la suta Zar! Hai cali de Zar! Keztra is Zar!"

The entire occurrence was breathtaking and compelling to watch. Michael would have never been one to believe in such practices, but he had an open mind through anthropology to understand varying cultures demanded different doctrines and means by which such doctrines were practiced and preached. He could tell Keith was enjoying it too and surprisingly so.

The three men running around in circles finally came to a stop in front of the altar. The crowd stopped humming as well, while they paid attention to the three men with differently colored blazing torches. The humming turned to chants repeated with the exact wordings and in the same manner over and over and again. The words were audible and disturbingly so because they kept on repeating it without end.

"Che Key Ta Zar", the villagers chanted.

The last word was understandable to Keith and Michael and it meant they were chanting to their god obviously. The three men with the torches lifted them up into the air and above their heads. They joined the burning torches together to create a brightly burning blue flame. It was amazing to watch. Keith leaned towards Michael.

"Remind me to take samples from those burning torches after the ceremony," he whispered. "This is fucking awesome."

Michael had wanted to say the same thing. His thoughts were on the amount of data they could collect from those fiery torches, the idea was exhilarating to think about. He nodded to his colleague and agreed without hesitating.

Farama's voice broke their concentration; "Wai he ja Howli!! Che key ta Zar!"

Farama danced around for a moment before stopping abruptly to place his twenty-foot long torch into the blue burning flame the other three men held. His torch now also glowed with a blue fiery light. He then arched the torch above the woman on the altar. Over her head there was an immense unlit torch. Farama set it ablaze. The burning light of that immense torch now illuminated the entire grounds. It was entertaining, and Keith was close to clapping then thought better of it.

Keith had a lot to tell his colleges and friends if they ever got back to his world above. The issue of how they planned on returning home hadn't been discussed between himself and Michael. The ship didn't currently function, and it was a sensitive topic with Michael, so they had not spoken a word about it since they landed in the terrain. Keith wished they'd speak about it though. He wished they would talk about it once in a while in their conversations, it was too scary to think about the future and what it might entail. All that mattered at the moment was the work they were doing.

The sound of beating drums suddenly alerted Keith to what he was missing. The crowd yelled in excitement. The coordinated rhythm of sounds tore through air. It was loud and hypnotic.

"Zar!" the villagers yelled again before the sound of their loud bass humming voices filled the air once more.

"I wonder, how long have they worshipped their god Zar? How long has this world existed down here below the earth?" Michael whispered to Keith.

The sound from their humming voices increased and the drumbeats heightened the process. The drummers, whose presence couldn't be seen cloaked themselves in the darkness of the night. They did their bit to make things really entertaining to those watching. Michael and Keith could barely manage their excitement as they envisaged what would come next.

The sound of the trumpet blared out loudly for a length of time, then the note of the horn faded away into the night, only to come alive again in the same note over and over again, this happened six times. On the seventh note however, this time around, the trumpet blared aloud in a higher tone, sending the previously humming crowd into a state of immediate silence.

With the silence came the sudden tilt of heads upwards to the sky by the villagers. Keith and Michael followed in their actions as they looked skyward. One of the villagers cried out. "Zar!"

The group pointed skyward as they pointed up in the night. The entire crowd resumed their prayers. The chants grew louder and more aggressive along with the drums beating in the background.

"Ohooh! Ahhh! Zar. Zar. Zar," they continued to chorus wildly and loudly.

Michael and Keith still were lost on what was going on until something caught Keith's eye.

"I thought you said this was all legend. A story." Keith said with bewilderment.

Michael looked around, "Yes, it is."

Keith shook his head.

"So then in God's name please explain that," Keith said.

He looked at the northern part of the sky and pointed. Michael followed the line his hand provided.

Michael couldn't see anything past the full moon in the sky. He strained his gaze as best as he could, but nothing seemed to be changing. He was just about to give up until a winged man flew by. Michael wasn't aware he had gotten to his feet in reflex to how shocked he was. The winged man flew in the firelight and sent the entire crowd of villagers into cheers and shouts with the words;

"Ohooh! Ahhh! Zar. Zar. Zar!"

Michael still could not believe his eyes, it was the same winged man he had seen depicted on the wall in the room where Farama had taken him. There was no doubt about it, but he still refused to believe. He rubbed his eyes in hopes he was seeing correctly.

"Is that Zar?" he managed to ask.

"Christ! Can you believe this?" Keith sounded more excited than Michael was.

Michael had no idea on what to make of their discovery. He couldn't believe his eyes and from the widened state of Keith's, he couldn't either.

"Helen Caldicott," Michael muttered.

Keith looked lost, "What?"

"Helen Caldicott, are you familiar with her? The Australian physician?" Michael sounded surprised.

Keith shook his head in decline of such knowledge, Michael shot him a disappointed look briefly before deciding it was no use fussing over it.

"She once said we're curators of life on earth and that we hold it in the palm of our hands," Michael quoted the lady he had read so much about and learnt from. "I never really understood the concept until now."

They both looked up to see the winged man land on the altar after hovering above it momentarily without making any sound. He bent slowly towards the woman in blanket and like a father he lifted the woman into his strong and powerful arms.

"What on earth is going on?" Keith couldn't help himself.

Majestically, he flexed his wings wildly in the air a couple of times in preparation for his flight before taking off with the woman perfectly held in his grasp. He flew high into the air, before circling around the group of men with torches before ascending into the sky and flying north a few seconds after. Michael tugged at his shirt, "Let's go Keith… come on!"

Keith felt reluctant to move, "Michael wait!"

Michael shrugged and got to his feet, "I have to go where he goes. We cannot wait here."

Keith grumbled and got to his feet too. He waited for Michael to lead the way and he followed behind him. They left the area where the villagers continued to celebrate their god's presence to run into the woods before them. The chase was wild and difficult, and it came with some bruises and the occasionally running in to branches and tripping over tree roots extending out from the soil.

"Shit!" Keith cursed and swore on various turns.

Michael tried his best to keep the winged man in view while also trying to stay safe. He had badly bruised his elbow from a rough fall which he had to scramble quickly to get back up. He could hear Keith continue to curse and swear behind him, both of them were getting banged up but he didn't really care about that; what mattered was keeping this creature in sight.

Michael had gotten too distracted by the flying winged man's movements to see a large trunk in his path. He rammed himself hard into it, causing Keith to do the same. Running at that rate of speed he was unable to control his body and they both fell. The sharp pain Michael felt in his leg was immeasurable.

He needed a few seconds to gather his focus once more before getting up, but to his dismay, the winged man was nowhere to be found.

"Where did he go Keith? We cannot lose him," he declared, yanking Keith's arm to help him up so they could continue on their chase.

"I'll meet you up ahead past that clearing," Keith said to him while making sure he could still keep the flying winged man in sight.

Michael tried moving but found that his knee was throbbing with pain. He had also sprained his ankle badly in the fall. He returned to a sitting position to nurture his injuries. The pain was unbearable. He had just bent forward when he felt blood dripping from his forehead. He hadn't realized it at the time; there was a deep gash on his head from the fall.

"Come on Mike," he urged himself to his feet.

The knee proved difficult to walk with, but he wasn't going to remain there. He just couldn't stay while Keith pursued the god alone. He limped towards the clearing where Keith asked him to meet. Keith stood in the middle of the field with the bright rays of the moonlight illuminating the entire area. He heard a soft sound of a twig snapping and turned around startled to see Michael limping over.

He rushed over to assist his friend, "I can still see him, right there he's a dot in the distance just above the horizon to the left of the moon."

Keith pointed into the distance. "There is nothing out there but mountains. He must be headed to a high ledge or in a cave or something."

The confused men stood and continued to stare into the distance unable to comprehend all that was going on. They've been there for months after traveling through a hole on the surface of their own earth only to arrive in another world underground with its own sun, moon and even the stars. They've seen things that shouldn't be possible and now a god with wings. "We must be dreaming right?" Keith said in bewilderment. "How is any of this possible?"

Keith had his hands on his waist and his eyes looked at the sky above. He waited for a reasonable explanation to every anomaly they've witnessed so far.

"Maybe this is where dreams come from Keith. This might just be the world of dreams," Michael uttered after a moment.

The two men stood in the clearing a moment staring into the starry night sky.

CHAPTER ELEVEN

The mood around the camp since they left the temple hadn't been one to celebrate. Yes, the discovery had been awesome for them all to think about and acknowledge, but maybe too much for one person in particular. It wasn't as they had expected it to be. It was naturally overwhelming, but the resulting actions were troubling, and they needed to find a way to get things right again pretty soon, before things would or could get a whole lot worse.

Reena had seen it first. She had her suspicions after seeing the rings of unrest around the man's eyes a day after they left the temple. It was morning and she had decided to reach out to Roland for something when he came rushing out of his tent, looking jittery and pretty much shaken like he was on drugs or something. She stared hard and long at the man, wondering what devil had gotten into him, but decided against reading too much into the scholar's actions.

She wondered if she should have just taken note of things then and probably informed the others. Roland looked a mess from that day onward. He barely kept his hair clean, and pieces and crumbs of the previous night's meal could often be seen on his clothes while some hung in his hair as if he didn't care on his physical appearance or if he was still sane.

He barely slept since the discoveries in the cave and barely interacted with the others unless he needed something important. She didn't know the man well, but she worried for his safety. He was going to burn himself out.

Roland didn't seem to care though. He didn't seem to be

interested in anyone around him, or in whatever they had to say. He would walk past, give a nod or grunt in greeting, and disappear into his tent occasionally and not come back out again for lengthy hours. Everything seemed to be messing with his head. Everything troubled the man.

"If I can just translate it... if only I can figure out how it is being translated," Roland was often heard murmuring to himself.

Then, he insisted on moving down there into the temple to be closer to the work. Two weeks passed and if it were not for keeping in contact via the radio, they wouldn't know if Roland were alive or dead.

Whatever phase he was passing through, it was beginning to tire Reena who needed to speak about it.

It was noon. Zachary toyed with his pocket knife, trying to keep his mind occupied when Reena cut in with the tone of her voice.

"Are you sincerely telling me you aren't worried about the doctor?" she began.

Zachary made no move to look up or even look in the direction of Reena. He had heard her obviously but wasn't willing to go down this path again with her. He simply wanted the time to himself to really think. His nonchalance irked Reena, who took away his knife forcibly from him, so he would acknowledge what she was saying.

"What do you want me to do Reena?" he sighed.

"He is obsessed Zachary and I'm wondering why you don't seem to see it! When was the last time you have seen him sleep? He looks like shit."

Zachary finally looked in Reena direction.

"He's a man on a mission," Zachary grinned.

"This must be his process, the way he gets things done."

She frowned immediately and rammed his pocket knife back into his hand.

"This is your fault," she pointed her finger right in his face. "You should have never agreed to let him live down there. Ralph said he caught Dr. Misthos talking to one of the corpses in those coffins last week."

Zachary truly didn't see anything wrong. Roland had been remarkable with his insight and the explanation he had given on his thoughts and the possibilities of what they have discovered.

"From the moment I brought him in Reena, I was sure we got the right person for the job, and he is one of us now", Zachary tried calming the lady down. "This is just the taste of something bigger coming and I can feel it in my bones, if we can just leave the doctor alone to do his thing, I'm sure all will be well."

His words sounded selfish, but Reena didn't need to tell him that. Her gaze told him all he needed to know already. "Make him return to the surface this evening so he can get some air. Staying down there too long isn't good for him." Reena suggested.

She really worried for the man. Sleeping in the temple just wasn't the way to live a healthy life, and besides it creeped her out that he slept down there with those mummies. As much as she needed answers, she didn't want Roland to go mad.

"Okay, maybe he'll spend the night in his tent today. He deserves it from the hard work he has been putting in", Zachary nodded. "I'll go down and get him myself if I have to, I promise."

Reena nodded in appreciation, but she wasn't going to be fine until she actually got to see Roland back on the surface and not spending the night again in the temple.

Zachary was a bit annoyed as he made his way into the temple. The climb down always took longer than he expected, and he was sure Reena was overreacting as usual.

He hated to think he was being a typical man dismissing Reena's concerns, but Roland was a professional after all and this was nothing but a man being excited about his work.

The work is what really mattered. He had just discovered what will most likely become one of the new seven wonders of the world. All the research and years of sacrifice Zachary had gone through will finally be worth it.

Not to mention the money, most of their money came from Digcorp, a cultural resource management company, or CRM. Money which is now running dangerously low. He would be lucky if he had enough money to last until the end of the month.

Soon, they will be able to finally leave this godforsaken desert and return to the world with fortune and glory. They all had their part to play and Roland's job was to decipher this strange new language, perhaps even unlock something new.

Zachary's feet finally touched the ground. After undoing the harness, he began making his way through the different chambers looking for the doctor. Zachary called out to Roland but there was no answer.

Roland had named them "the rooms of knowledge," and Zachary felt it had a nice ring to it. He continued his walk into the room until he got into the third one where Roland had himself too engrossed in his own thoughts to even realize Zachary had waked in.

Zachary took a good look at the piles of books in the room which ranged from being four feet high to less. It felt good to see he was totally vested in getting answers but the cubical formation in which he arranged the books around himself were somewhat creepy. Zachary called out to Roland.

Dr. Misthos! Roland?" Zachary called out to the man to gain his attention, after coughing gently but to no avail.

He didn't move an inch, but muttered, "Gara ta ze dotay."

Zachary stared at him in disbelief and somewhat perplexed manner as to why he didn't hear. He cleared his throat louder and clapped his hands together before yelling the man's name to get his attention. It worked, as Roland slowly turned around.

His face was unshaven. A full beard covered his face. Roland was wearing his glasses which makes his eyes seem larger than normal. His clothes were dirty and worn and Zachary could tell that a bath had escaped Roland for some time.

The smell was almost unbearable. Zachary also noticed that Roland has lost some weight since the last time he had set eyes on him.

 Zachary could see the absence of sleep in the red eyes, but it wasn't the only disturbing thing; the man had lost some weight too. It had been two months since he began his work in the temple, they communicated more through the radio and Zachary thought that was enough. He didn't expect what he was currently looking at, a man on the brink of madness. The odd sight made him take a few steps backwards.

Roland waited for the man to speak. He wanted to get back to work this man was wasting his valuable time.

"I didn't mean to disturb you," Zachary stammered as he cleared his throat.

The doctor took his time to answer. Zachary didn't realize the man wasn't consciously with him. Part of Roland was somewhere else.

With intermittent blinks, he finally answered, "Oh, Zachary, I wasn't expecting you. It is good to see you," he sniffed before he continued. "I'm sorry I've really been busy, how can I help you?"

Zachary thought of stepping closer but decided against it. "I was wondering if you wouldn't mind coming to the surface to share your report with me."

Roland looked bothered and annoyed, "Is it really necessary at this moment? I mean-."

"Yes, it is Dr. Misthos. Ralph found something really interesting that should help our pursuit so far," he interjected.

Roland looked around the room and the work he still had to comb through.

"Do we have to do it right now?" he asked in a rather disappointed tone.

Zachary nodded to the man. "It will take us at least an hour to climb back up before they can pull us up with the winch the rest of the way."

Zachary could see how badly Roland wanted to remain in the temple, but from the disturbing sight of things, he couldn't let that happen. The man looked like a drug addict waiting for his next fix. Roland did indeed need a break from the work. They needed him in pristine condition with a sane mind and not the half-crazed person that stood before him. Reena was right. Zachary had gotten there just in time.

With some reluctance, Roland nodded in agreement. He got up from his seat grudgingly and began to pack the eighteen handwritten black and white marble notebooks carefully stacking them into a rucksack. He closed the rucksack gently and held it close to his chest like a mother would her beloved child in hopes of preventing the child from harm. He looked around to be sure he wasn't forgetting anything or leaving anything important behind.

Zachary waited for him. Seeing that Roland had everything he needed, he placed a hand on Roland's shoulder and forced a smile before finally speaking, "How are you feeling doc? How are you really feeling?"

Roland managed a wry smile, "Great! I feel fantastic because there is so much to learn here, and I cannot wait!"

Zachary nodded and led him to the exit.

"We will discuss everything when we get to the surface Dr. Misthos... You can enjoy a cool bath and a good meal fit for a King once we get back to the surface," he urged the man on.

Roland didn't stop talking about the discoveries he made. His words ran endlessly and painfully so with gesticulation and weird actions that made Zachary turn around to look at him.

"Are you sure you're feeling well Dr. Misthos?" he felt forced to ask.

"What? Ah, yes, I'm sorry. I was sounding like a mad man, wasn't I?" he chuckled loudly. "I'll explain everything at... wait, what meal are we having?"

"Dinner Dr. Misthos... we are having dinner," he replied to the man whose grip on time was slipping.

The doctor nodded gently, "Yes, dinner, and I will explain as much as I can then."

Zachary realized the doctor wasn't really talking to him, Roland was talking to himself. He kept on murmuring inaudible words and tasking himself with questions that made it seem like he was about to explode. He asked himself a lot of questions and kept on answering them a moment later. Zachary could begin to see what Reena's fears were as the man barely had his harness on until Zachary intervened. The realization was troubling.

Zachery was trapped between his feelings of guilt for allowing the man stay and wither away down in the temple for that long, as well as feeling a sense of joy about getting answers to questions he needed. He was just a few hours from being able to get his answers, and he could not wait.

CHAPTER TWELVE

The main tent was decorated with a bulk of Ralph's drawings from the temple. The man had spent hours trying his best to replicate the majority of what he saw in the temple and he wasn't doing a bad job. There were no pictures, Zachary had been intensely afraid of using modern cameras and video equipment.

He knew flash photography and regular plain old light could damage the artifacts that he and the team had discovered because the pigment used in the parchment tended to break down under visible light.

It's the same reason why a newspaper will fade and turn yellow if you leave it in the sun. Imagine the damage one could do to parchment that had been buried in the dark for hundreds of years.

If the parchment was suddenly exposed it to light, the artifact could be destroyed.

As tedious as it was, that is why Ralph was painstakingly copying the scrolls and artwork by hand. Even handling the scrolls with your bare hands could damage it because of the oils on your skin.

Roland had just walked in after getting himself cleaned up with a nice bath and some fresh clothes from his trunk. He looked lanky in the clothes which were now a loose fit around his body. He hadn't paid attention to them until he got into the tent where the others were staring.

"It is good to see you Dr. Misthos," Reena said. The others greeted him as well.

They gathered around to have their meal. With his trimmed beard and fresh clothes, he looked better than he did earlier. They commenced eating their meal of koushari, a vegetarian dish, that is made up of chick peas, lentils, rice and macaroni. It tasted unlike anything Roland had ever eaten before. It was truly a mixture of different civilizations and cultures all one on plate. It tasted just heavenly and Roland couldn't help but eat the filling meal with gusto, he had not realized just how hungry he was and his body seemed to demand the nourishment. He took a pause from his meal to feel his trimmed beard and also take note of the absent of his glasses which he had taken off. He felt naked without it.

He looked up to see Reena staring at him, only to take her eyes off of him once he looked in her direction. Susan and Zachary occupied themselves with Ralph who continued to crack them up with jokes. The group finished off their meal with shai, a mint tea local to the area and baklava.

Roland figured he needed to join the conversation; "I must look atrocious."

Reena looked up abruptly, "What?"

He pointed to his beard, so she could see what he was talking about. The trimmed looking mass of hair brought a smile to Reena's face. The voices of Ralph, Susan and Zachary laughing away filled the tent.

"You don't like the beard, do you?" Roland finally asked.

Reena shook her head to decline his notion. "On the contrary, I think it looks nice."

She allowed herself to smile again before looking away shyly and into her half empty plate. Roland sipped his tea while eating his dessert of baklava but was surprised when he found himself still looking around the table for something else to eat. He stopped to check out how lean he was looking tugged at the shirt on his body. He felt like he had been tossed inside a sack.

"I cannot believe how thin I got while I was down there," he lamented while checking himself out some more. 'I think I went a bit too far this time."

He sighed and felt their eyes suddenly turn to look at him. None of them had told him how horrible he had looked before the bath and how gaunt he was at present. He figured they didn't want to hurt his feelings, but still, he would have loved to know.

"This happens every time I set my mind on getting something done. "I must look like a crackhead," Roland mumbled discouragingly.

The man's words about how much weight he had lost made Reena laugh out loud. She laughed hysterically, breaking the tension in the room. After a moment, her laughter mellowed and settled in to a genuine smile once again. She maintained her gaze solely on her plate while Roland looked up at her.

"Here I was thinking it had something to do with my cooking." she teased.

Roland shook his head immediately, "No, it definitely cannot be your cooking... I love your cooking."

He wasn't lying about loving her cooking. It was one of the first things that got him comfortable with the environment when he first arrived. He had thought meals here would be hellish and prepared his stomach for the worst, but surprisingly, that wasn't the case and with that came some good comfort too.

 "Well, you must be dying to know what I've been doing down in the temple for all this time." he cleared his throat.

Zachary sat back into his chair and looked relaxed, "Yes, it has crossed my mind as well as others too."

Roland inhaled deeply and exhaled duly. He sat back into his chair and rested himself well enough before crossing his hands over his chest.

He picked up one of the black and white marble notebooks that he always seemed to have with him and opened the book, double checking his notes he closed the book and smiled.

"When I first tried to translate the language, I could not make heads or tails of it, it didn't read like English writing from left to right." Roland explained.

"Then I thought it might be a form of tategaki where the Japanese characters are written in columns and read from the top to the bottom and then the columns themselves are read from right to left." He described further.

Roland got to his feet and paced the tent as he spoke.

"Maya script and Egyptian hieroglyphs are written in rows or columns and can be read in either direction pending on which way the animal figures or human figures are facing." Roland clarified.

The group nodded to indicate they were all following his train of thought. Roland paused then continued.

"That is when I noticed these lines!" Roland walked over to one of Ralph's reproduction of the temple's walls. He pointed to what he was talking about. The assembled group nodded in understanding.

"At first, I thought they were spacers separating words, that however wasn't the case. After days of study and contemplation, that is when I saw it. Do you see it?" Roland asked.

From the blank stares and silence in the tent, Roland guessed the answer was no, he continued with his explanation.

"The lines form a pattern, a pattern than can be found in nature!" Roland smiled then told them the answer.

"It's the Fibonacci sequence! Its nature's numbering system and can be found everywhere. The scales of a pineapple, florets of a flower and even in a grain of wheat! It's meant to be read in a spiral like this."

Roland demonstrated with a motion of his hand, "starting with zero and one, the sequence is zero, one, one, two, three, five, eight, thirteen, twenty-one, thirty-four and so on," Roland stated.

"Once I figured out the pattern, deciphering the language became possible."

"There are still quite a number of symbols that look foreign to me and might take time to understand, but I've been able to begin translating what I can read." he scratched his head shyly.

The latter part of the story was obviously what Zachary had been waiting for. His eyes widened in excitement, and his lips tore apart with a wild smile.

"You did it! You actually pulled it off!" Zachary chuckled and laughed wildly.

Zachary upped himself from the seat and yelled in glee to show just how glad and excited he was for the discovery. He turned to Susan, lifting her from her seat and kissing her wildly in celebration. His joy was immeasurable.

"What does it say? Your translations, what exactly does it say?" Reena questioned.

Roland walked towards her. "Well I translated the right panel in the first room. It's a more detail version of the scrolls you found."

He pulled out one of the worn black marble notebooks and flipped through a couple of pages while Zachary calmed himself down under the instructions of Susan, who also happened to be his wife to hear what Roland had to say about the translation. He finally got to the spot he wanted and paused.

"Yes, here it is, I need you to listen to this," Roland asked of them before he began to read the translation that read and sounded like broken English;

"In the beginning of time, life was good, and with it was harmony, in which every race on earth lived through. Among us are men of power. Some are with us, while others want to destroy us. It was Trosiat, the great ruler of the world that kept the peace. A long life did he live and although it was believed that he was immortal, he was not and passed on.

With Trositat gone, a void was created. The creatures of the earth became divided; trusting only those within their race. There were some who remained as one. That group came together and left this earth to live in Yaardau deep below the earth. Then the war broke out; each race trying to win over the other, so Yahweh became angry and flooded the world.

The world of Earthtar was destroyed forcing a scattering of the races. Yahweh then let the races begin again. The peace didn't last long, and war broke out again, but this time Yahweh did not inter-fere, and many years passed. In the end the race known as the hu-manidauns won the war. It was a shock to the other races because the humanidauns are weak creatures with short life spans. Yah-weh loved them for their simplicity.

It was a cruel joke to some of the other races in which some had the power of dreams and could destroy many humanidauns; twice as many came again like a plague and they sought to wipe out all the other races more powerful or different from them. So, began the 1000 days of Bosaler."

Everyone remained still momentarily and said nothing. They tried to relate with the story in their heads and battle through what it was all about exactly. They spent the next minute thinking hard but to no avail. They were lost and had nothing to go on.

Zachary broke the silence as expected of the man, "Who is Bosaler?"

Susan piped in as well, "And Yahweh? Who is Yahweh?"

Reena was expecting the question and knew the answer. "Yahweh is the Hebrew name for God," she answered.

Ralph cut in immediately, "Are you saying these beings believe in God?"

"What about the war? What war is that exactly?" Zachary cut in again.

Roland didn't say anything. The questions he had been asking himself in his head were being asked by his colleagues. So many questions with no answers. They rung in his head and with it came a deafening sound like white light. He tried focus, but it felt harder with every try. He could hear Zachary ask more questions, but his voice sounded muted as if he were under water. Something was happening to him, but he couldn't figure it out. He felt his consciousness slowly begin to ebb away.

His hand let go of the book first, followed by his knees buckling and the sudden slump to the ground.

"Quiet! Shut your mouths! Stop asking him questions!" Rena yelled upon realizing something was wrong with Roland. "Quickly, come and help me tend to him!"

"What is wrong with him?" Ralph inquired.

Reena took time to respond as she bent closer to Roland, "He's going into shock!"

Roland hadn't lost his consciousness entirely the room seemed to close in on him. His vision went blurry. He continued to stare at the lot trying to help him. Reena lifted him and held his head close to her chest, while she rocked him gently. She looked terrified and worried.

She continued to rock him while the entire room fell silent. Roland felt his body shudder violently. Are they still asking him questions he wondered to himself? He tried to answer them, but he could not hear his own words.

"I don't know... I don't know... I don't know," he continued to mutter endlessly.

Susan cleared the path of bodies before her to bend close to Roland. She parted his slowly closing lids to look into his eyes, he continued to mutter the same words in soft tone over and over and again. He saw a flash of colors and the darkness took him.

It was a few minutes after midnight and standing underneath the shining moon was Reena. She stood at the edge of the desert oasis gazing at the moon's reflection on the surface of the water, where it bounced off it beautifully. The sound of a struck match startled her into consciousness.

The familiar sweet odor of the Macanudo and the intake of smoke from the Dominican cigar meant she wasn't alone and that Zachary was behind her. The man puffed some more from his cigar before walking towards her.

"How is he?" he asked.

She was hoping on having some alone time to clear her head but that wasn't going to happen. "He is sleeping now, but he doesn't remember anything about losing it earlier."

"I'm sure he will be fine," Zachary spoke without sounding troubled or worried.

His nonchalant demeanor enraged Reena and he could see it in her eyes.

"How on earth is he going to be fine? None of us is ever going to be fine again!" she vented loudly. "I don't want Dr. Misthos working on this project anymore!"

Zachary shook his head.

"It's not like you to share my fears of what might happen to our world. You surprised me. Twice in one day. Since when do you know the Hebrew name for God?" he said sarcastically.

"You're killing him Zach!" she cried. "He will crack under the pressure!"

"It has already begun Reena and you cannot stop him... I forbid you to try to stop him! I have to know! He has to know! That's why he was the way he was tonight. I need to know because I fear the future. He needs to know just to know! Besides what about finding a cure." Zachary sounded stern.

He walked towards her and stood at her back to whisper slowly into her ear.

"What about finding a cure. It's what you have been fighting for. Five years ago, you came to me. Remember? I wasn't going to put you on the team, but you fought and won your spot. We can't stop now. Dr. Misthos will continue to translate the walls and you will help him. The answer to life itself could be written on those walls!"

"What if we don't like the answers we come to find?" she spoke without looking at him. "What if your worst fears come true?"

Zachary shook his head and tossed the cigar away, He tucked his hands into his pockets and looked away from her.

"May Yahweh help us then." Zachary walked away slowly.

He left Reena with her thoughts.

CHAPTER THIRTEEN

The breaking of the dawn came with the beauty of the sun like none they had seen or that they had simply taken note of since they arrived in the strange land. It rose majestically over the mountain tops, coming to life like a new child and sending its ripples of magnificence in the form of golden rays. The mountains look different today too, with their gray and black color blending perfectly with the white snow covering the majority of the peaks.

In a nearby cliff, a strange animal flew overhead, catching Michael's attention before Keith's. The creature was a gorgeous sight to behold, and swift in its movement as it gracefully flew around them. It looked like a bird, however it was no ordinary bird. It bore a resemblance to a ferret with multi-colored wings.

It flew a little too close for comfort and Michael was forced to chase it off momentarily with his hand. He managed to pull himself up the side cliff while scaring the creature away, turning over to Keith he stretched out his hand out to the man.

"Give me your hand Keith!" he called out.

Keith struggled but he managed to reach out towards Michael grabbing hold of his hand. Michael put everything he had into the action. It was slow and painful and felt like his arm was about to be pulled out of its socket, but he finally succeeded. The entire episode was starting to look and feel like a bad idea. They definitely hadn't envisioned it turning out this way.

With their backs resting against the wall of the cliff, they panted loudly and aggressively, trying to catch their breaths. Michael couldn't talk much; he didn't have anything to say just yet, but

Keith obviously did. He looked infuriated and tired at the same time.

"When I got this job, I believe I may have been grossly misled", he hissed and spat. "The freaking ad said they were hiring those with five years of research experience and not fucking rock climbing."

He looked really irritated as he felt every part of his body ache. Michael seemed to be enjoying the entire thing. He smiled and chuckled annoyingly at his friend's dilemma.

"Next time read the fine print," he said sardonically.

Keith shot him a disapproving look before sighing. He decided to get even when the time comes, but they had things to sort out at the moment and it was about time they got it done.

"Do you think that next cave above us is it?" he asked looking up.

Michael looked worryingly at the cave with mixed thoughts; "If it isn't, then we are dead. We've been up here for six days and we are almost out of food."

"Well you know what they say, ninth time is a charm," Keith said.

The menacing wind blew hard once more, making them cover their eyes. When the winds died down they looked back up towards the cave in which they both hoped would be the right one, otherwise it would have all been for nothing.

Michael sighed "Well if I could fly I would probably pick the highest cliff too."

"How high do you think this ridge is?' Keith asked.

Michael took another look upwards to evaluate how high it could be. He took his time and did the math in his head.

"I will say about seventy-five if I'm correct", he guessed. "I cannot be certain for sure, but it looks like it."

Keith took a good look himself before turning around to look at Michael, "You have got to be fucking kidding me!"

He couldn't believe the mess they had to go through.

"I wish I were," Michael said before gulping down some water.

Michael pointed ahead, "See that ridge over there? We will climb up and set up camp for the night there."

He hadn't even thought about where they were going to spend the night before Michael mentioned it. Seeing the environment crawling with weird animals, Keith didn't want to spend another night out in the wild. If the animals didn't get them, then the cold would.

Worried Keith shook his head and continued to sulk.

"I'm not sure we should continue. Maybe we are not meant to know," he advised his friend.

Michael moved close to console him. "It's not much farther I promise. Besides I need to know."

Nodding towards Michael and stretching his arm before in a grand gesture, "Lead on!" Keith said.

They began the tireless and joint aching process of climbing farther up the ridge. Michael didn't dare stop. He was running on pure adrenalin and was running low on juice. Keith struggled on but wasn't doing bad either and eventually they both reached the top of the ridge.

"We need to start unpacking to make camp here for the night," Michael taking the situation in hand.

Keith shot him a disheartened look. He hadn't even had enough rest, yet the man was talking about unpacking and setting up camp. He helped himself to some water from his bottle, before returning the ration into his pack. He looked at the dirt laden ground and got lost in thoughts.

"Mike!" he called out. "I've been thinking a lot about the past eight months and… ", he paused.

Michael put down his pack to approach Keith. He looked tired.

"And what Keith? What is going on with you?" he sounded worried.

Keith looked away; "This is crazy!"

"What do you mean?" Michael said looking confused.

Keith explained. "When the tremors started. We came to investigate what was causing them. Then the quake hit. The ground opened up to reveal a fork. I expected to find some really rich soil samples maybe a new deposit of gold or oil. We found an entire world! We are over 7000 feet below the earth's crust and I'm climbing a mountain. There is a moon and stars above my head! It's fucking impossible!! Now we are on a quest to find a winged god!"

"I know all of this is overwhelming, "Michael started to say.

Keith cut him short, "Overwhelming! Mike listen to yourself! Then listen to me! We are underground! How the hell can there be a moon and a sun and animals and a race of people down here! It goes against every damn thing I ever learned!"

Michael was at lost too. He wasn't going to deny the fact that he was, because it was the truth.

"I don't know what to tell you. I don't have the answers you seek. All I can say is look around you. We are both here. This is not a dream."

Michael encouraged Keith to take a good look around, which he did grumpily. It truly wasn't a dream and they could feel it from the cawing sounds of the birds in the distance, to harsh feel of the mountain wind brushing past their skin. All their senses told them that it was all real without doubt. Keith wanted to keep believing it all, but his brain kept reminding him that all of this went against the laws of physics. Was it real or just an illusion that felt so real. The thought was disturbing.

He turned to Michael, "What if we're dead and none of this is real? What if we're trapped in some kind of purgatory?"

The struggle between his brain and spirit fought back and forth for control.

"What if we already died even before we hit the ground?" he continued.

Michael approached Keith without any prior warning, grabbed hold of his arm and squeezed it badly until the man yanked it way in pain.

"If you felt that, then it means we're alive," he shot back.

"That means we are very much alive and well. We are here! Maybe we had all the answers to life when we were children. Maybe what we dream isn't a dream but a thought or a piece of something we lost a long time ago."

He flung his arms into the air before suddenly pausing.

He realized Keith wasn't listening to him any longer. He seemed engrossed by something else. Keith looked past Michael as if he wasn't standing there. Michael turned around in curiosity to see what his friend, whose face was now pale, and eyes wide with shock was looking at. Michael gasped and took a few steps backwards.

Before them was the winged man standing and looking at them. His appearance was silent, and his presence was somewhat intimidating. They had no idea on what to do or how to address the strange being.

As they drew closer the figure became clearer, His age was impossible to tell, he didn't look old, but he wasn't young either. He was possibly the most fit being they had ever laid eyes on. He was muscular and tall with wavy blonde hair and striking blue eyes. Raw power seemed to roll off him in waves and the two men were almost compelled to fall to their knees in submission. The robes he wore were so white that they seemed to give off their own light. There seemed to be a hidden strength to him, the graceful way he stood, his posture and of course the enormous beautiful white and grey wings that adorned his back. There was a glow in his eyes that seemed to light the feature in his face and a depth in his gaze that surpassed anything resembling human.

Nudging Michael hard, "Say something," Keith urged him. "Maybe he speaks the same language as the villagers."

Michael didn't know what to do, instead he opted to use a simple form of sign language mixed with English. He was simply out of his depth.

He pointed at himself, "Hi. I am Michael."

He repeated the gesture while pointing at the winged man as well, but they got nothing in response.

"You... Zar?" he pointed at the figure and asked.

Upon hearing his name, the winged man blinked and smiled at them both.

"Do you think he understands you or anything you're doing?" Keith inquired.

Michael shrugged gently, "I honestly have no idea, but he is smiling, which is good."

Keith decided to speak with the winged man; "Hello... Please forgive my manners, but I've never met a god before and to let you in on a little secret, I'm terrified as hell."

Michael waved at Keith to stop talking. The winged creature looked at them once more and smiled.

"Hello," the winged man said to their surprise.

The men exchanged a brief and nervous look with one another.

"You speak English?" Michael said in surprise.

Zar nodded; "You two are from above... you are both humanidauns. How did you get here?"

They were lost on what he meant by humanidauns but Michael did the honors of explaining about the earthquake and how it created a canyon that led them to the unknown world.

"Hold on one minute, but are you Zar?" Keith interrupted.

"Yes, I am," Zar acknowledged with a nod.

"Are you a god?" Keith bluntly asked without realizing he had just done so.

Zar waited a few seconds while looking around before responding, "It depends on what you mean by a god," he replied in a rather subtle tone.

Michael and Keith shared a brief look as a million thoughts and questions ran through their minds.

"Before I continue, I know you have numerous questions running through your heads, I have just as many questions to ask you as well," Zar continued. "Let us take you to where we dwell, with your permission that is."

Michael raised a brow and leaned his head closer to the winged man. He wasn't sure he had heard correctly, and some clarification would be needed.

"Did I just hear you say we?" he inquired.

Zar held in his hand a pale-blue crystal and raised it as high as he could just enough for it to be in line with the sun. The sun connected with the crystal, the light from the sun magnified its brightness causing it to glow twice as bright. The crystal began emanating a beautiful blend of sounds unlike anything they had ever heard before. It was a melodious tune that filled the air and touched the soul. It almost brought tears to Michael's eyes.

It didn't take long when the flapping sound of wings greeted them from the distance. A beautiful radiant woman flew above them. Her landing was gracefully but still terrifying. Her presence startled both men.

Keith cleared his throat, he examined the angel like creature before him. She was by far the most attractive person Keith had ever laid eyes upon. He was at a loss for words in her presence. Her peaceful celestial demeanor encouraged him to step closer. She seemed fascinated by their presence as well and her deep blue eyes seemed to bore it to Keith's very being. Michael and Keith stared at her in wonderment. The silence that followed started to become uncomfortable.

She looked to Zar to provide a valid explanation of what was going on.

"I know you must be confused, but they are humanidauns from above.", Zar explained to her in a subtle tone.

The winged goddess examined the men. "Let's take them to the dwelling place quickly before someone sees us."

Diaona had her eyes on Keith. Her gaze was piercing, she smiled at him.

"Come. We mean you no harm. Turn around and relax," she encouraged him. "You should enjoy the ride."

Keith slowly turned around, so his back was to Diaona.

Diaona wrapped her arms around Keith's waist firmly and with it came the realization of just how strong she was. Zar approached

Michael who was more willing than Keith, to do the same thing. They approached the edge of the cliff and took one look at each other and then to the men they had tightly bound in their arms, before leaping off.

The drop was terrifying for them both. The gods simply chuckled and smiled at each other during their descent with their wings folded and tucked in to place along their backs. Keith screamed the most while Michael tried his best to remain calm even though he was screaming in fear in his head. The gods suddenly spread out their wings catching the wind and slowing their descent. Keith had begun swearing inaudibly.

They soared back into the sky at lightning speed, feeling the wind brush against their cheeks in the process. It was exhilarating and equally frightening, but it felt wonderful and Keith screamed wildly and shouted as if he were on a rollercoaster back home. Michael remained calm and was just happy he had not pissed in his pants. Now that they were gliding across the sky he enjoyed the ride with Zar.

"Oh my God! I'm flying... I'm flying Mike, see... I'm flying," Keith screamed.

"They are the ones flying, and we are just along for the ride!" Michael bellowed in the ear deafening wind.

Keith didn't care, he enjoyed the ride with the gods.

"Where are we headed?" Keith asked Diaona.

She simply smiled at the man without giving a response. She dove into the air as did Zar, to Michael and Keith all the mountain tops looked the same. Cold and foreboding in their size and presence.

However, one mountain peak, the one off in the distance, the one they seemed to be headed for looked broken, maybe broken is the wrong word to use. Instead of coming to a point like the other mountains, this one had a huge crater at the top. It would have been impossible to see from the ground, but up here among the heavens it was clear to see. They continued flying until they arrived seeing an opening at the top.

The opening revealed the most beautiful garden either of them had ever seen before. It was magnificent in design and lush with trees and fruit. The grass looked green and full of life, they could see the ferret-like creature they encountered earlier flying around without a care in the world. Hopping and flying from tree to tree.

"This is amazing!" Keith exclaimed.

The winged gods carried Michael and Keith in to what is known as Ailedin Valley. The view is biblical, in the sense that this beautiful garden could very well be the Garden of Eden from the book of Genesis. It looked like paradise. The villagers did call Zar, God, is this what the bible wrote about? The implications were daunting. Could this be the divine garden in Zion? Michael thought.

 The word Zion and Zar, was it a coincidence? In the book of Genesis, Cherubim or angels were placed in the garden with a flaming sword to keep everyone away from the tree of life. The two men were indeed being carried by what seemed to be angels.

 "You need to brace yourselves humanidauns," Diaona warned them both. "Pull your knees in slightly towards your chest and get ready to hit the ground running before finding a means to slow yourselves down."

Keith nodded his head in agreement. The four of them successfully made their landing and the men did exactly as they had been informed.

"This isn't real... I mean, this cannot be real," Michael muttered, racing forward to feel some of the leaves.

Zar and Diaona looked at the man and smiled.

"This is beautiful! This is freaking incredible!"

Everything Keith had seen so far clearly defied everything he had come to learn in his life. It defied all logic.

"How is all of this possible?" the man inquired. "I don't understand any of this."

"How could you? All of you have forgotten, even with the sacred sites to lead you," the female god stated. Her words puzzled Keith and Michael. "Sacred sites? What are you talking about?" Keith asked.

Zar shared a quick glance with Diaona and they both spoke in their native dialect. Michael shrugged and stared at Keith who also seemed interested in knowing what they were talking about.

"Diaona! This is too much for them to take in all at once! Please hold tongue! Prepare the Star Chamber's outer room for them to stay in." Zar cautioned her in their native tongue.

"Forgive my sister's rudeness. She has a way of being overly expressive and she needs to learn there is a time and place," he grinned. "We have so much to discuss but you look weary and definitely in need of some rest."

"I think we both can use something to eat and drink, but I need to ask one question first." Michael uttered.

"By all means ask." Zar declared.

"How is it you know our language?" Michael said, wondering what the answer would be.

It was a really good question. It was one Keith wished he had thought about so he could ask it.

Zar walked towards them with his hands held behind his back. He stared into the beautiful skies and took his time to collect his thoughts before answering.

"I learned it when I was a child," he briefly answered.

Michael couldn't understand how they could learn the language being spoken on earth or where he had learnt about it from.

"It is essential for us all to learn languages especially those belonging to your kind, as we all knew this day would come to past," Zar stopped walking while speaking. "I will gladly answer more of your questions after dinner."

He urged them along in hopes of showing them around.

"Come... Come and see what has been missing from your lives," Zar asked of them.

Keith was more enticed and excited than Michael. The valley extended for miles ahead and nothing was in sight with the exception of a single structure, which could be seen off in the distance. Diaona made herself scarce almost immediately by flying into the air in one powerful flap of her gigantic wings.

She needed to get there ahead of them, so she can prepare the structure. She wanted to make sure the one she carried to Aliledin, Keith was comfortable. She wanted to please him, but she didn't know why and that thought made her nervous.

CHAPTER FOURTEEN

Reena has been spending her days and nights with Roland helping him decipher the new language. The language itself was like a giant puzzle, most people are often perplexed and daunted when confronted by a puzzle, not Roland, he immersed himself completely.

In the beginning when you often start a puzzle the pieces are a jumbled mess, the same can be said for a language. Any language not known to you is a puzzle, as you expose yourself to it you pick up pieces of a conversation, or see a certain phrase written in a certain way and it becomes a mystery that needs to be solved.

It is human nature. We strive for order and balance. This is what Roland did, his mind was uniquely wired to solve puzzles. It takes a methodical thinker who can see things mathematically and sequentially.

Roland had discovered that the spacers led the way to how the text needed to be read using the Fibonacci sequence, however unknown to him until a couple of days ago was the fact that the spacers were also mathematical equations. Essentially there was a language within a language. It was like putting together a 3-D puzzle on crack and Roland loved it.

The smell of books filled the room, and the only sounds that could be heard were from pages being flipped. The tomb chamber of the Temple of Goulaumx was now another place they could call home.

All of this time with Roland was finally paying off. Reena now spend most of her hours reading what Roland had been writing down in his notebooks. She sat in the chamber, flipping through the pages of the seventh book Roland had successfully tran-scribed. Slowly, she absorbed the content one after the other, while Roland remained in the fourth chamber not too far away from her. She could hear him scuffle around at times when she listened attentively for his movements. Roland was aware of her presence, sometimes she would catch Roland staring at her but when she asked him if he needed anything he would just smile, apologize and walk away.

Roland had just finished drafting his twenty-ninth book when he felt the need to call for Reena; "Reena!"

She jumped up from her seat, closing the page she was reading carefully, "I'm coming Roland! I will be right there."

She hurried away from the table and trotted over to the man call-ing for her. She hastened her steps and arrived at his room looking worried.

"Are you okay Roland? You sounded a bit tensed when you called," she inquired in concern.

He nodded and managed a weak smile, "Yes I am, and sorry I called you so suddenly. I have a question about something I need to find out."

The suspense was killing her, and it felt as if Roland was taking his time to study her from where he sat. He turned to look at Reena slowly from his chair, with his eyes beaming with unsaid words, he wanted to speak but something held him back.

"What is it you want to know about Roland? Are you sure you're okay?" she stepped closer to talk to him.

He got up from his chair and looked around as if he was worried they were being watched. He went as far as to ensure Ralph wasn't in one of the rooms close to theirs, before returning.

"Can I trust you Reena? Can you assure me of your trust?" Roland sounded paranoid.

She didn't know what to say, then simply nodded.

"Of course, you can…," Roland interrupted her.

"I need to know because what I am about to tell you cannot and must not leave these walls," he warned sternly. "At least not until I have done more research."

"You can trust me Roland… you know you can," she assured him.

Roland could tell she meant it, but some circumstances still prevented him from speaking out. "What about Zachary? Will you assure me and give me your word that he wouldn't be involved or hear about any of this?"

Reena didn't hesitate before nodding; "Yes."

She waited and watched the man think things through.

Roland figured he needed someone he could trust within the camp at least and one he could share his ideas and findings with.

"Have a seat. Let me tell you what else I've discovered," he urged her towards the empty chair opposite of his.

"This is so inconceivable, I can hardly believe it myself," he cast his gaze down and away before looking back up. "Do you remember the first time you came down here to begin learning the language and the texts with me?"

She couldn't forget it even if she wanted to. She nodded, "Yes."

Roland cleared his throat, "Do you remember that symbol you stumbled upon? The one that we couldn't find a meaning for?"

She nodded.

Roland implored her to listen to the words he was about to read out loud. He picked up a marble notebook and flipped to a marked page.

He began;

"There came a day when our numbers were few in the world and the knowledge was kept secret. Those of us that decided to stay above worked to help the humanidauns remember the art but as soon as it was taught to them, their life force would end. Others used the knowledge to gain more power over the ones who were not given the secret. In fear of another war, only the chosen were taught. Then the fear rose up again in the humanidauns, this time against their own kind. Anyone who practiced the art was killed. The humanidauns were forgetting everything. The story of our past was written as legend. Then fantasy. It was decided that the only way the humanidauns would remember is through Sacred Sites of Heruby."

"What are the Sacred Sites of Heruby?" Reena asked.

.

"Think about it Reena... think about those things in the world which we cannot come to give adequate explanations of," he urged her to follow his path of thinking.

Reena drew a blank. She was at a loss for words.

"The Pyramids in Egypt, Stonehenge in England… think about all of them Reena," he encouraged.

Their conversation wasn't going anywhere. She began rubbing her temple. Confused she gave up.

"What on earth are you talking about Roland? I honestly have no idea on what you are trying to say," she confessed.

He got up and walked to the corner of the room where he had large rolls of maps stashed. He picked up one of them and spread the map on the table.

"Take a look at this." Roland stated.

The table couldn't contain the entire width of the map, prompting Reena to take it from him and spread it on the ground where they could have a better view without issues. He smiled at how resourceful she was, before getting down on his knees as she had done. They both shared a brief smile before getting back to business.

Pointing at a section of the map; "See! This is where the pyramids are and where you'd find Easter Island. All you need to do is connect the dots here and there."

He assisted his teaching with the use of a pencil, matching the points on the map one at a time as he described on to Reena.

"Oh my God!", she exclaimed.

Roland nodded, "Yes, it is the same sign."

"What does this mean," she asked.

Roland smiled as he spoke, "These people, our ancestors had ideas and practices that are separate to both science and religion."

"They had access to a power that has been long forgotten then later considered myth. They used techniques and forgotten words of power to bring about change in the physical world, simply through the force of one's will!"

Reena just stared at him in shock. Roland continued. "It's been known as shamanism, transtheism or sorcery. Simply put, it is, in all its forms. Magic. They used it to create another world below this one!"

Reena shook her head vigorously, deciding it just wasn't possible.

"That cannot be true.", she voiced. "It cannot be."

Roland asked her why she couldn't believe it. "According to everything in here which I translated, it appears that the use of ancient magic helped create a world people could live in."

She wasn't buying any of the things he had just told her. She wondered how he had even stumbled upon such nonsense when it wasn't the main point of their objective in the chamber.

"I don't want you taking this the wrong way, but what you're saying is insane and the fact you even want to believe it feels insane.", she sneered. "It's not logical or possible. It's a matter simple science. You can only dig so far before you hit the mantle. You have the top layer that we live on, then the lithosphere, asthenosphere, mesosphere, the outer core and the inner core. Jules Verne's book is just a story. It's not real."

"I believed that too until I discovered all of this." Roland expressed.

He got up and walked away from the floor where they had knelt for the past few minutes. He walked over to the writings on the wall before stopping to trace a symbol in the air with his hand and muttering in a strange language Reena had never heard before.

Eijdo apar hodilar.

With the mention of the words came a loud noise and a flash of blue light which began to hover above his head gently. He stood firm. She stared at the bright blue light in awe.

"Come here Reena," Roland asked of her.

Reena shot up from where she was previously kneeling. Moving closer without taking her eyes off of the blue light above Roland. She was baffled as to how the man could summon such an oddity out of the air.

"How… how… how did you…?" she stuttered.

She tried gathering her strength to ask the question.

"How did you do that Roland?" she finally got the words out.

"This is just the beginning and it is why I need you to keep this between us," he replied without looking at her. "That why Zachary can't know. Not yet. Not until I understand everything. I didn't believe any of it until now."

Reena continued to look at the magical light. She never believed in magic and always saw it as some flimsy trick meant to delude the stupid, but this was real, and Roland never looked like the kind interested in cheap tricks.

 "It's going to take some time. Study! Learn with me and together we can unlock the secrets of the universe!" he smirked.

He looked too excited and unable to contain himself. He felt glad having someone to share his discovery with.

"Why do you trust me with this? You could have kept it to yourself." she shrugged.

"It is a feeling I have when it comes to people and I see you as someone I can trust," he told her.

"That's a little dangerous, don't you think?" she warned, sounding unsure of herself.

"You were there for me Reena... You stood by me through the hellish months and cared for my wellbeing," he stared deeply into her eyes.

She took another look at the blue light above his head, a smile growing across her face.

"You can trust me Roland. You can count on me," she assured him. He nodded gently.

CHAPTER FIFTEEN

Paradise is a place where animals and humans are in perfect harmony with nature and God. The breathtaking views, perfect weather and crystal-clear waterfalls certainly make it seem that Michael and Keith have indeed found paradise. Not to mention that they are walking and talking with what appears to be living breathing angels. Keith keeps feeling his chest to see if he has a heartbeat, just to make sure he had not died and go to heaven.

The night was beautiful and the entire Aliledin Valley, where they were currently located, was absolutely breathtaking. Keith was captivated by the sight of it all, while Michael embraced the scientist in him, and did his best to commit every image to memory in hopes that he would be able to analyze the data later.

Zar watched the humans with some degree of curiosity, as they continued to marvel at the world around them. He could not blame them for being so enamored with their surroundings. Could the stalemate truly be coming to an end? Zar wondered to himself. It was obvious to him that they knew nothing of the war or for that matter anything of their history. Ignorance is bliss. He didn't need to burden them with the knowledge yet. He would let them enjoy the valley.

Michael cleared his throat and smiled, "This place is a paradise."

The wind howled through the trees, creating a beautiful melody as the branches and leaves danced and swayed against each other. It was like in organized symphony, the melody unlike anything any orchestra group in his world could conjure.

Michael sighed as he took in the landscape all at once, Zar

watched him, a thin smile escaped from the corner of his lips as he observed the human.

"Yes Michael, we love nature over here and this is what...," Zar paused suddenly losing his train of thought as something caught his attention.

Michael watched something he could not identify run through the forest. His eyes widened in surprise. Realizing he had no hope of identifying the creature, he turned back to Zar.

'You were saying something before you stopped," Michael reminded Zar.

Zar pondered before responding, "I'm sorry but I cannot recall what I intended to say."

Keith suddenly joined in on their conversation.

"Who would have guessed gods could forget anything?" Keith pointed out.

Zar chuckled at him. "Well, as you can see we aren't exactly gods," Zar noted.

Michael held his chin gently and looked around to ascertain what Zar might be talking about.

"So, you're just beings that can fly?" Michael responded in affirmation rather than trying to ask.

Zar responded with a nod. He turned around and looked across the entire forest, Zar walked up to a strange looking blue flower. He patted the petal gently and with it, the stem grew wings, uprooted itself from the soil and made its way into the air before going to settle in another fresh portion of soil far off from where they stood.

Keith looked dumbfounded. He had never in his life seen anything like that before, was it a flower or something else? Keith looked around for plants of the same nature, before doing the same thing he had seen Zar do to them. One after the other, they slowly uprooted themselves and flew off to find a less disturbing environment to settle in.

"If you aren't like me or my friend here, then what exactly are you?" Michael inquired while speaking to the god whose back was turned away from them.

Zar shrugged before replying, "Many years ago. Probably centuries for you. The ones who were not like us, wanted to be us."

Keith who wasn't paying attention to the conversation was now roaming around the forest like a child in the playground. It amazed Michael on just how childish his friend could be in such times.

"What happened to your kind or to those who sought to be like you?" Michael urged him to continue with his story.

Zar sighed intermittently as if the events happened days ago instead of centuries ago.

"It was a horrible time for my kind... it was one shrouded in chaos as darkness."

Sadness filled Zar's eyes as he retold his tale.

He finally looked at Michael to speak, "It was the worst time of our lives and I can recall it like it had happened yesterday. They killed us for our wings... they captured, tortured and killed us for the wings which they could not use. They wore them as clothes or tried to brew potions in the hopes of transforming themselves."

"Why didn't you fight them off? I mean, you look like you could hold your ground in a battle or at least fly away from the danger to places they could not harm you," Michael suggested wondering why that wasn't an option.

"That would have been possible, if we had been a violent people," he replied. "We preach peace and calm we never give into aggression, it impossible for us to fight back."

Michael finally saw the dilemma. He couldn't imagine himself in that kind of situation. Having to make the decision not to fight against the opposition and instead trying find a peaceful solution or die trying.

"Some of us got away, but there were others that were not so lucky, and they got caught and were dealt with. The horrors like nothing I had even seen," Zar noted.

He led Michael and Keith forward as silence filled the air. Michael's thoughts consumed him as he went over the situation they were in. To live through such horrors, but the human race has always dealt with violence and war. He wondered why they were even being invited into such a beautiful valley given the circumstances.

"So why trust us?" he aired.

Zar smiled as if he had expected the question, "You're from above. If the prophecies are true, the time of waiting is over."

Michael was definitely confused this time around. He took the opportunity to look in Keith's direction before looking back at Zar. Too many questions filled his head. Zar seemed to read his thoughts.

"I know you have questions. Zar smiled. "Soon all your questions will be answered."

They journeyed forward through the forest with the moonlight above guiding them through in its beauty. They came to a halt in front of a large stone structure shaped like a frozen tear drop. Keith stretched his hand towards the structure to see what felt like when Michael slapped his hand off in caution.

He frowned at Michael's action but couldn't do anything about it.

Zar distracted them by speaking, "This is where you will be staying. I hope you find everything you need. In the morning we will talk. For now, rest."

"Where will you be sleeping?" Michael asked.

Zar smiled then stared into the sky. He flapped his powerful wings and leapt into the air soaring into the canopy of tall trees above until Michael and Keith lost sight of him.

They stood there and admired his ability for some time as they looked up in to the sky.

"I wish I could fly like that," Keith said before accompanying Michael towards the teardrop structure.

Enthusiastically Keith walked briskly past Michael and into the structure. He was momentarily caught off guard as movement caught his eye, they had not expected anyone to be in the structure, fixing a table filled with varying kinds of food atop it was

Diaona. He approached her without making his presence known. He had just gotten a few feet from her when she turned around startled.

"Oh my... you startled me," she gasped.

Keith tendered a bow in apology before looking around.

"You two move faster than I thought you could," she added.

Michael cut in with a slight smile, "We may only have legs and no wings, but they but they get us to where we want to go."

Diaona looked down in shame on what she had said, Keith stepped closer to the lady and gently placed his hand to her chin before leading it up. She had read Michael's words wrongly and he needed to intercede.

"He was only joking at your expense," he informed her. "We cannot thank you enough for all you've done."

She nodded and quickly lifted her head up and walked away from the men and headed for the door with her hands in her front she shyly looked at Keith.

"I will leave you two to your meal now," she said a shy smile.

They waited for her to exit the room before turning around and having a brief look at one another. Michael placed his bag to the ground gently before gently crouching into a sitting position reminiscent of the Native Americans with his legs crossed over one another before the banquette and without further ado, he began eating.

Keith shot him a baffled look and yelled, "What in the heavens do you think you're doing?"

Michael was slightly startled, and he took a brief halt to look up and answer the man, "What does it look like I'm doing? I'm eating."

"I don't think we should be eating Mike. I don't trust Zar and my gut keeps telling me not to," Keith noted.

Michael took a good look at the meal and sighed, "Why don't you trust him?"

Keith shrugged and walked to the door to take a quick look outside. He looked around to make sure there was nobody eavesdropping on their conversation. He was content to find no such persons outside their door before turning back to continue his conversation with Michael.

"I think he is hiding something," he pointed out. "He is holding something back."

Michael nodded in agreement, "I know he is, but we can do nothing but wait till morning. I know you don't trust Zar but you seem to trust Diaona who went through the trouble of making the meal."

Reluctantly, Keith looked down at the food prompting him to slowly take his seat by Michael and begin to eat. Michael watched him pick up the first piece of food and stuff it into his mouth. He won't admit it out loud, but it was good.

It was one of those moments where Michael would have loved to laugh out loud, but he kept himself from doing so.

Muttering underneath his breath so Keith would not hear, he said,

"It is the child in us that loves."

CHAPTER SIXTEEN

It was a typical day on the Army military base as it prepared the next group of recruits for Basic Combat Training or BCT as it is known among the other soldiers.

The goal was simple, to take these out of shape civilians and transform them in to combat ready soldiers. Some succeed but most of them fail.

It's an experience not soon forgotten. The four in the morning wakeup call will start the day with a two-mile run, calisthenics and formation marching.

 A man dressed all in black and barely visible in the darkness walked past a squadron of men getting yelled at by their drill instructor.

 His thoughts go back, many years ago when he was a soldier. Its seemed like that was a lifetime ago, he knew by nine in the morning there would be the scent of puke and bile on the wind as half of these newbies throw up last night's dinner and their morning breakfast.

He actually caught himself smiling at the thought. These guys have it so easy, they just have to do what they are told and follow orders. They won't be burdened by the daily decisions that have to be made to keep this country safe.

Tonight, they will actually get to sleep. Dark blissful sleep for at least a couple of months until they take their first life, then their soul will be forever broken, their fate sealed in blood, its true what they say, ignorance is bliss. Then the few that will still be able to sleep after that, will be like him. Those few will get recruited into other sectors to do the work that most people can't do.

The man was like a shadow as he made his way across the base. He finally arrived at the building he wanted to go to and stepped inside.

The general's office was a simple room. The walls were adorned with a couple of simple landscape paintings along with a framed photo of the general shaking hands with the current Commander in Chief.

There were two couches, with a couple of uniformed officers who occupied the space discussing strategy and logistics and behind the large desk towards the back of the room sat General Dubner, a menacing looking man in his late fifties, he was still in excellent shape for his age.

His hair and moustache have that salt and pepper pattern that made him look distinguished. He was going over a map in detail on his desk. The man in black watched and waited to be acknowledged. The other men in the room didn't even see him enter and won't remember when he left. He was a shadow.

The general looked up at the man. "Mr. Levine." Levine answered the General in the same tone.

"General." There was an uncomfortable pause between the two men.

Even as the General looked at Mr. Levine, you could tell there was something dark and unsettling about the man not easily put into words. The flat black color of his eyes matched his black raven like hair. There was a malevolence in his face that made the room seem cold and a darkness that seemed to always surround him.

Levine continued. "The ship is almost ready."

"How do we even know, if the damn thing will work?" Dubner snorted. Levine responded to the general question, his voice hissing out like a snake made the general's skin crawl.

"McLoughlin and Weber aren't engineers they had help. We found out who helped them and now he is helping us."

———————

Somewhere in a remote area on base, hidden by some foliage is a bunker. One solider stands at attention with watchful eyes scanning the area for anyone or anything that is not supposed to be there.

The bunker was designed to protect people or valued items from attack, at first glance it looked like a small structure.

Perhaps something you would store weapons in or an electrical compound but what was seen was just the entrance, most of the structure was imbedded sixty feet underground.

The bunker in actuality was a ten thousand square foot compound with fifteen-foot-high ceilings. The outer concrete walls were thirty feet thick and heavily reinforced with rebar.

Nothing could get in or out unless the powers that be wanted it so, today nothing was getting out, not even the violent agonizing screams that came from within.

Gary Marks was welding a piece of metal to a craft that looked like a miniature submarine with folding wings on each side. Gary was a good-looking beefy man whose callous hands and toned arms suggested he was a hard-working blue collared gentleman.   A person who worked with his hands. His bushy red beard matched the top of his head, but the man looked like he was in pain. His face was bruised, and he has a black eye. occasionally, he looked at a video monitor, his eyes swelled up with tears, "The fucking thing will be ready in less than twenty-four hours! Please, I beg of you, let them go!"

He didn't want to believe that they could be so sadistic. He tried hard to keep his focus on the task at hand, but he could not concentrate. He couldn't help it, and he had to look back at the monitor which bore the sight of his wife, young and still in her mid-thirties, and his little girl, who was only eight years old. They were innocent in all of this why would someone do this he thought.

"Please let them go!" he pleaded in a softer tone.

His wife and child could be seen sitting in chairs with their backs to each other. Both tied with heavy rope and gagged cloths in their mouths. Every now and then a cattle prod would come in to view of the monitor, threatening violence, the electrical clicking and popping along with his family muffled terror filled screams drove Gary to his breaking point.

Gary couldn't take it any longer, his anger turning to pure hate filled rage prompted him to get to his feet and rush toward one of the guards closest to him.

"You son of a bitch!" he yelled at the top of his voice throwing caution to the wind.

He shoved the large armed guard against the wall, attempting to disarm him of his weapon, but the effort was futile. The guard easily overpowered Gary hitting him in the head with the butt of his rifle and reopening a bloody gash on his forehead. Gary fell to the ground.

"You fucking piece of shit!" The guard kicked him hard in the stomach and sent him tumbling backwards.

Gary struggled to hold what little food he had in his stomach, the sudden pain and lack of breath was too much, and he instead retched and vomited all over the floor. The gash on his forehead hurt like hell and the amount of blood now easing out of the wound temporarily blinded the vision in his right eye.

The guard approached him and yanked him by his hair as he dragged the bloodied man towards the monitor to look at it.

"Look at them Mr. Marks! Look at them and ask yourself, how long do you think your daughter and wife can take this," the guard sneered.

The guard tossed Gary Marks to the ground and yelled to another guard that was in a different room far away somewhere on the base but with a live video feed could be seen and heard on the other side of that monitor, occupying the same space where his wife and daughter were, it was like they were in the room next to him. "Taylor! Get this motherfucker to listen to reason!"

Upon hearing that order, Gary looked up from the ground and into the monitor to see what was going on. The other guard had a smirk of madness on his face. He gently took the gag off of Gary's wife's mouth, so she could speak.

"Oh my God, Barbara," Gary murmured.

Her first set of words came out as screams. Her deafening cries filled his ears. Tears ran down her face freely.

Barbara turned to the guard who assaulted her, "Why are you doing this? What have we done to you to deserve this?" She yelled.

Her questions got no response from the guard who simply seemed intent with torturing her. Muffled whimpers escaped from their daughter's lips. Barbara's pleas became more frantic, as she begged for mercy.

"She is just a little girl!"

Seeing that she had no effect on the guard in the room with her, Barbara turned and yelled in to the camera that was trained on them.

"Gary! Please help us!" she implored.

She had just spoken when the guard extended the cattle prod and struck her as the prod made contact with her skin sending streams of electrical shocks through her body causing her to spasm. Mark's wife screamed in pain and terror.

"Please! No! No more! Please Gary, no more!" she yelled, praying her husband heard her and could do something to end this nightmare.

Gary looked at the guard in his room, with tears in his eyes he tried getting himself into a sitting position. He reached for the monitor as if he could somehow touch his wife and daughter, but the guard kicked him in the chest, sending him sprawling backwards and back on to the ground in the process.

The guard leaned in closer to Gary and spoke in a malevolent tone,

"You just lost your viewing privileges!"

Through his black eye he watched helplessly as the guard turned off the monitor. The screen went black.

"A lot can happen within a twenty-four-hour period. Heck it took less time to start a war over in the Gulf. If I were you, I'd finish that fucking machine and finish it quick!" the guard spat out.

Gary slowly crawled back to the machine picked up the welding torch. With his face still drenched in tears and his hands finding some degree of stability he went back to work.

———————

Someone once said that to gain the advantage in something you might have to lose or do something harmful that in the greater scheme of things, might be considered less important.

In other words, we might have to do something that is not pleasant to gain something greater. There is however a price that must be paid, and the price is always high.

General Dubner looks at the men assembled before him. Once he gives the orders, there will be no turning back. Things will be set in motion.

 This is his last chance. Is it worth the price? He made his decision, or rather he came to the realization that he really didn't have a choice. The choice has already been made, he was just another cog in a big machine.

It was time. He looked to his left, Major James Malkin stood at attention waiting and Lieutenant Todd Porter to his right, He was ready to address the soldiers in front of him.

General Dubner cleared his throat to speak, "Good Morning Gentlemen. As all of you are now aware, we are just putting the final touches on a prototype ship that we will attempt to fly in to Devil's Fork.

This is a class two mission, so I am required to inform all present that nothing said today is to leave this room and is an act of high treason if this confidence is breached. Do all present understand what I have just told you."

The room remained silent as they agreed to every word stated except Mr. Levine who sat in a corner in the back of the room.

Continuing, General Dubner coughed gently, "Fine. Let's continue. A little over nine months ago we received a communication from scientist Keith Weber and Michael Mcloughlin with word that they entered Devil's Fork. We know that they were alive because they sent back proof of this fact. Since then we have not heard from them. Until just recently entering the fork was impossible. I'm proud to announce that we have obtained the knowledge to do, what the two scientists have done which is enter the fork without harm.

The General paused for effect before continuing.

"We also know that at the very least that there is some kind of a biosphere down there because animals and plant life exist. If that is the case we must also assume that there may be other forms of life as well."

The latter end to his statement brought a widespread of murmurs among the men as they tried understanding what he meant. Major Rattner asked the question that was on all of their minds.

"May I ask about what you mean about other forms of life being present General?"

The General turned to look at the men;

"It is as I said Bob, there might be other beings as in people down there," he explained.

The room erupted with some degree of murmurs again.

"That's why this has become a military mission. Not to mention that tension already runs high with the other super powers of the world. This is also a rescue mission as well as a fact-finding mission. So, let me introduce you to the two pilots," he announced.

Major James Malkin and Lieutenant Todd Parker stepped forward to claps and cheering from the men before them. They waved and saluted.

"Like I said earlier, this is a very sensitive situation. I have word from the President himself that under no circumstance is the media to find out anything," General Dubner warned. "This is the reason the ship will be dropped during a code 111."

He had just dropped a bombshell on them for the second time in one day. The men shifted uncomfortably in their seats. They looked around to one another.

Major Leto took the opportunity to speak, "Won't that set off a possible war?"

His words had definitely struck the right nerve in everyone. They felt the same thing upon hearing the code they were to follow.

The General raised his hands in the air to ease their worries, "That is a risk we are willing to take gentlemen. We have to be strong willed in such times."

"Who will take the fall?" Major Leto inquired.

He looked around and the others nodded, waiting to hear which group would take the fall for such hideous act.

"The Black Dagger, under a guise of a terroristic act we will enter unnoticed", the General noted.

Major Rattner could not take it, "Jesus Christ! You're not talking about a code 111!! Innocent American lives are at stake! What's the count going to be?"

It was an unspeakable act, personally he didn't agree with it but he wasn't the one pulling the strings.

The General responded, "Fifty-six maybe more."

The words sparked an outrage and continuous murmuring until the General called for decorum with his hands held high.

"Why not just bomb the damn fork!" Major Rattner suggested in a sarcastic tone.

"Look! This comes from the very powers that be! Please don't fight me on this! The stakes are very high and there can be no question as to what is going to happen! Is that clear! Good! Gentlemen you have your orders."

General Dubner took a long pause to look at the faces around before continuing.

"Now that we are all on the same page on this, I declare this meeting has come to its end," the General sighed.

His last words coincided with the men getting up from their respective seats and filing towards the door and out of the room in somber mood with the exception of General Dubner, Major Malkin, Lieutenant Porter and Mr. Levine.

Mr. Levine who was almost forgotten stood up and walked over to the three men. His gaze drifts towards General Dubner. General Dubner looks down towards the floor at his shoes, suddenly it becomes abundant clear who is really in charge.

Mr. Levine approached Major Malkin and Lieutenant Porter to speak with them, "Once you get in the fork, if you find Weber and Mcloughlin kill them. You have twenty-four hours to digital visual record as much as you can then return home with the intel. Is that understood?"

CHAPTER SEVENTEEN

What is this feeling, this emotion that is like surprise but deeper, it's that feeling of knowing something very rare, something unexpected, but it is more than one emotion, isn't it? That feeling for joy, respect and fear all mixed together like a stew in a pot.

The more you add the better it will be. It seems almost silly to name this feeling. Michael thinks to himself as he sits and takes the situation in. He is in absolute wonder, and by the look on Keith's face, he is too. What do mere mortals do when surrounded by gods.

The morning in the strange dwelling felt different from their previous nights in the new world, the two decided to get some fresh air in the beautiful garden that is the Aliledin Valley.

Michael led the way as they journeyed deeper into the gardens. Both men were lost in their own thoughts.

Michael in particular wrestled with his emotions. Without realizing it, he had come to a tipping point where his knowledge and science no longer applied, and it perturbed him.

He figured eventually, if he collected enough data, he would be able to explain how all of this was possible. He hated the word because of all the negative connotations that came with it, but Michael was an atheist. He didn't believe in a higher being controlling his fate.

He was a simple man of science and in the past, he was always able to explain, the what's and the way's using logic, math and the scientific method. It always came down to the systematic observation, experimentation, testing and then formulation and modification of those hypotheses.

Keith gasped, breaking into Michael's thoughts. The two men spotted a creature human in appearance but small, it wasn't any bigger than the size of Keith's hand with fairy-like features perch high atop a tree branch. The creature smiled at them, waved then flew away. The two men stared in amazement until they lost sight of it in the branches above.

They kept silent and continued to enjoy the moment until Keith decided to break the silence.

"And you said we didn't die. It sure looks like heaven to me," he turned to Michael with a wry look on his face.

Michael shrugged and looked around some more. His gaze taking in the beauty of this place.

Michael chuckled, "Going by that rational, you realize we went in the wrong direction and could be in the other place, right?"

Keith looked around again and shrugged this time around. "Well, if this is Hell, then let me burn!"

Michael laughed softly and plucked a flower from its root before beginning to examine it closely. It felt soft and feathery, and he could almost swear the plant was moving in its hand like it was alive. It's not logical his reasoning told him he was handling a plant and not a human life. This place didn't make sense to him. Annoyed he dropped the flower letting it hit the ground,

Taking his attention away from the plant, "It is peaceful here isn't it?"

Keith sighed and nodded, "Yes, it is."

The two men enjoyed a calm tranquil sense of being in the new world that was unrivaled by anything they felt before landing here.

"Do you realize it's been over nine months since we have made contact with the world above?" Michael stated as a matter of fact.

It was one of the things he thought about in the night before he went to bed. He wondered what was going on above and if any attempts were being made to come for them. He often entertained himself with endless scenarios on the message they sent and what the world must think. Either way, there was no way of knowing. Keith must have been thinking about the same thing because his voice echoed Michael's thoughts.

"Does it bother you that they might not have gotten it?" Keith asked.

Admittedly, Michael did every now and then entertain the idea that no one may have gotten their message but quickly dismissed the notion when he did the math. It wasn't just a rocket that they shot up in to the air that day. It was a miniature version of the ship they used to get into the Fork. Keith didn't completely realize it, but it was a distress beacon with triple modular redundancy built in to it. It had more than enough fuel to make it out of the fork, the on-board computer would keep it from crashing and the hold compartment held their digital recording plus the live specimen. Even if the specimen didn't survive the trip, it would still provide proof of their discovery. The only logical reason they didn't receive a message back after all these months is either everyone is fighting for the right to come down in to the fork or the government received the message and is keeping it secret. Either way he looked at it, it was still troubling.

"I don't know if it went through Keith, but I often think about whether they got it. What do you think?" he asked as he raised an eyebrow.

"We sustained too much damage during the landing and I don't think any of our equipment was salvageable. Two days after we sent the message that fire destroyed most of what we had," Keith recalled.

Michael nodded briefly, "Yes, but we could assume the professor got the message... maybe someone will come through the fork like we did and try to find us."

"I don't even think they could get down here for a while, it might take them a year or maybe two, depending on how many intellects they have working on this. Half of the design of the ship I got from a Fantastic Four comic!"

Michael could not argue with him on that and he nodded.

"What about Gary?" Michael pointed out. "He is the only one who knows about this but what if he talks?"

Keith shook his head fervently, "By now with the money we gave him he and his family must have moved to Indiana to live on that farm he always wanted."

Michael after a moment nodded thoughtfully and agreed with Keith assessment. Looking out into the perfect gardens, Michael's thoughts suddenly darkened with a realization.

"Do you think we should warn Zar about the possible dangers?"

Michael asked with uncertainty.

Michael had just ended his sentence when the sudden gust of wind greeted them from the south.

"What dangers should you warn me about?" Zar asked in person.

Zar had glided down quietly enough through the air and flapped his wings to sail down to the ground without making a sound and now stood next to the two men. It was a feat Michael didn't think was possible with those massive magnificent wings. Zar held in hand a crystal and looked from Keith to Michael and then back again.

"I don't know about here, but in our world, war is a common occurrence, our mere presence here might be disruptive," Keith noted.

Zar looked at Keith wryly and shook his head. His gaze seemed to peer into his very soul, "I see you don't trust me Keith, do you?"

Keith was trapped in between giving a sincere answer or giving one which he thought Zar might want to hear. He cleared his throat and looked over at Michael once again before looking back in Zar's direction.

"I just don't understand what exactly is going on," he finally responded.

Michael finished Keith's sentence, "Pardon us Zar. We are... In the dark on a couple of things."

Zar shook his head, "It is I who should be making the apologies and asking for your forgiveness. I have truly kept, the two of you in the dark long enough. It's about time for you to have the answers to your questions. This should help.

They watched Zar gently sat on the ground. Carefully holding the crystal in his left hand in front of them to see. Then Zar tossed the crystal in to the air, as it came back down, it suddenly halted in midair hovering and levitating before them.

Keith smiled wildly and continued to stare at it in amazement, "This is really crazy! Can you believe this?"

Michael nodded immediately and smiled. He felt like a child watching some kind of magic trick. It nagged and pulled at his mind. The logical and scientific part told him what he was seeing was impossible and yet, here it was happening right in front of him.

"You took the words right out of my mouth Keith," Michael finally responded.

The crystal began to glow brightly, it seemed to pulse and shift as if it were alive. It almost seemed to be moving, no it was more than that, it looked like it was beating, beating like a human heart. Just as Michael was about to mention this fact to Keith, the crystal began to spin and rotate. It was hypnotic. Keith must have felt the same thing because it felt like he was being pulled towards the crystal and even though Michael could not look away from the light of the crystal, out of his peripheral vision, he could see Keith trying to brace himself. The light grew brighter and filled his entire vision. He heard himself breathing heavy, Keith too. Was he hyperventilating? He didn't feel scared and yet, Zar's calm and commanding voice broke in to his thoughts.

"Do not be afraid. Look into the crystal and clear your minds. It remembers everything, and it will guide you once you allow it the images to come to you," Zar instructed.

Michael did as Zar had instructed while Keith managed to keep his focus on the crystal as well. The longer they stared and focused on the crystal, the brighter it glowed before it began moving slowly between the three of them in a manner that made it almost impossible for Michael and Keith's eyes to keep up with.

The two humans remained enthralled by the crystal. Suddenly there was a bright spark that flooded their vision until they could see nothing but the blinding light. Slowly, their minds began to delineate out images which they were certain they had never seen before.

The images came into their minds like a flash of lightning one after another. They seemed to have a three-dimensional quality to it. The images started out small and far away and grew larger as it came closer to them. The best way to describe it would be as if someone had thrown a baseball directly into their faces. The images seemed to slam into their minds, leaving an impression behind. Then everything went black. Michael blinked looking around. He felt like he was on the verge of something fantastic, some idea or memory that was on the tip of his tongue. He looked at Zar who seems to be pre-occupied by something or someone. Keith! Michael was suddenly aware that Keith was with him but lay unconsciousness on the ground a couple of feet away from him.

"What happened?" Michael leapt out of his Zen like state to look around the garden.

"You are fine Michael, you need to keep calm," Zar assured him.

138

Michael looked over to Keith who was twitching in a disturbing manner on the ground.

"What did you do to him?" he asked. "What happened to us just now?"

Zar reached his hand towards Keith to check his pulse, "He is simply taking longer than he should, but he will come around. We need to wait for him to come around."

Michael didn't know what to do. He was helpless as he watched his friend's body shudder and spasm uncontrollably on the ground. It seemed like minutes were passing by, but Michael knew it must have been more like thirty seconds, but it felt like an eternity. It took longer than anticipated but Keith eventually snapped out of it.

Keith looked around with wild eyes and in fright, trying hard to ascertain what was going on around him.

"What is going on? What is going on Mike? Did you see that? I mean...," he vented and continued to breathe hard and abnormally.

"Calm down Keith! Keith! Calm your nerves and you will be alright," Michael tried assuring him.

"You will be fine in a few minutes," he assured Keith.

Keith rubbed his eyes as best as possible, "What in the heavens was that?"

"Your memories enhanced a thousand folds. What did you see? It is different for each person," Zar replied.

Keith looked at him and began stuttering, "Mea... mea... mean-ing... meaning we saw different things?"

Zar nodded.

"I saw everything... everything about where we are from, the birth and rebirth of the world... I saw everything!" Keith sounded aston-ished.

Michael was at a loss. He could tell Keith was expecting him to be able to relate with him. The experience he had turned out com-pletely differently for him.

"I saw nothing other than flashes, images I could not make sense of. I tried but it still remained blurry," Michael explained.

Keith was lost in his own mind, he remembered things he didn't do and knew things no man should know. He tried hard to focus his mind. Keith's facial expressions kept changing. At one moment he looked like he was about to burst out laughing, in the next mo-ment he looked angry with hate and disgust in his eyes. Heartache and sorrow followed as tears ran down his face.

"What is happening to me?" Keith cried out in confusion.

Michael looked over to Zar and his gaze demanded an explanation to what was going on.

Zar stepped closer to Keith and checked his eyes like a doctor would his patient seeing something Michael could not.

"He has an old mind or something in those images unlocked some-thing very old. He will never be the same again."

Michael had hoped he didn't hear correctly when he looked back at Keith, "What the hell did you do to him? What do you mean his mind would never be the same again?"

"What the hell do you mean by that!" Michael yelled What did you do to my friend?"

Zar explained, "I did nothing to him, but more to do with what he has done to himself."

Things just didn't seem to make sense anymore. Keith continued to look embattled and he wouldn't stop murmuring words incoherently as he stared at something only he could see.

"I thought we were going to get the answers to our questions!" he yelled.

"You were not ready for the answers you seek, but he now knows everything. He will get better once he begins to understand, his mind has to grasp the knowledge he has been given. It will take time to cope with what he had just seen," Zar said calmly.

Michael walked away from him and held Keith by his shoulders to look into his face. He wore a blank expression and his eyes held nothing in them.

"What did you see Keith? What did you see in there?" Michael demanded. It took some time for Keith to respond but when he did, his words were shocking to hear, "I saw God... I saw God!" Keith said in wonderment. Michael backed away from him slowly and gasped.

CHAPTER EIGHTEEN

It's just another typical day at the law firm of Ostroff, Kaufman & Fuchs. If you think about it, it's quite insane.

The function of any law firm is to advise their clients about their legal rights as well as represent clients in business transactions, civil matters and criminal cases.

The more complicated the better. They use language so complicated that regular people have no hope of understanding it.

So, you need lawyers who are fluent in legalese who can speak to other lawyers in legalese about things so mundane it boggles the mind.

Covering anything and everything. The firms fight each other with words and poorly written laws each trying to find a loophole that could give their side the advantage.

These battles could last months or years depending on what is on the table. What's on the table, you ask? Money. Lots and lots of money. They will battle until there is a victor or until there is nothing left on the table to fight over.

A man in a well-tailored suit walked into the office building and waves to his colleague.

Paul Wasser felt his neck and with it came a smear of sweat in a way he had not expected. He looked at his wet palm and shook his head gently in dismay, "Ken, its hot as hell in here!"

He got no response immediately, but Ken finally answered, "Yeah, it has been like this for a couple of hours now."

"What the fuck?" Paul turned around to inquire.

Ken shrugged and replied "Yeah, the AC is out again, but they say they are working on it." Paul gestured to his left.

A group of men no less than seven in count in jumpsuits with the name "Poland Air" printed on their breast pockets stood at the security desk waiting to get in so they can do their job.

Paul snorted, "If this keeps up, the next meeting we have will be in Cabo on the firm's dime!"

They laughed and opened the door to the conference room. Three other lawyers were in attendance and there waiting for Paul and Ken. Paul flung his briefcase into a nearby chair then walked over to a pitcher filled with ice and water and poured himself a glass. He paused to take a long refreshing drink then addressed the assembled group before him.

Paul cleared his throat, "Okay guys, this has to count, and we cannot do anything to fuck it up!"

He looked around the room for emphasis to see whether or not they were in sync with him.

"Okay this is the moment we have all been waiting for. This is the reason why we took the Bar.", he continued. "In less than two hours Mrs. Korn will be here and she wants something that will absolutely bury her husband.

Ken smirking spoke first, "Well let me just say we have something that she might like."

Ken looked pretty pleased with himself. He adjusted in his seat and fixed his tie properly, but Paul didn't seem convinced by what he had heard.

"No Ken. I don't want something she'll just like. I want her to have a fucking orgasm right here in this office! Joseph Korn is a United States Senator I want something that will guarantee at least 4.5", Paul mimicked Ken slightly while gesticulating with his hips.

His words and actions brought out a soft chuckle from the rest of the men in the room.

Ken dramatically placed his briefcase on the table while Paul straightened his suit and wiped the sweat from his face. "Damn it was hot in here!" Paul thought to himself and continued to look at the man expectantly.

"Then listen to this", the words were accompanied by the sound the of the briefcase lock opening.

 "In this briefcase are pictures as well as a flash drive with a digital 4 K recording of …," Ken sounded excited.

Paul cut Ken off and answered. "That waitress in Texas?"

Ken smirked, "Even better."

Paul took a guess speaking again, "A drugged out hooker from Broad Street?"

Ken shook his head and paused dramatically for effect. Paul raised an eyebrow that demand the information from him. Ken pulled an eight by ten glossy photo out of his briefcase and spoke in a spectacular fashion as if he was an actor on the stage.

"He had a romantic and lustful night with Douglas Escobar, a cable repairman by day and male dominatrix by night who goes by the name of Lord Boris and resides in Queens."

He watched Paul fall to his knees with his hands over his mouth while trying hard not to scream. Paul walked on his knees until he was in front of Ken.

He looked at Ken with his hands spread apart, "You are my god!"

Ken laughed out loud. One man in the room grabbed a legal pad from the table and wrote ten million on it then showed what he had written down to the rest of the group. They all nodded in agreement then the group of men mockingly bow their knees to Ken to mock him as the Numero Uno, Top Dog and Big Cheese of the law firm. If all went well, a few hours from now they would all be eating prime cut steaks and popping open bottles of Dom.

All they had to do now was wait...

Outside the glass conference room where Paul and his colleagues can be seen laughing and joking around before their big meeting, a delivery man walked off the elevator and surveyed his surroundings eyes sweeping around the floor as though he was lost. In his hands a large box of roses he has to maneuver and guide past people who are walking around and towards the receptionist. He swerved right and out of the way of a uniformed man who in a rush almost knocked the roses out of his hands.

"Good morning Sir, how may I help you?" the chubby looking lady behind the desk asked him before he got to her.

"Good morning, I have a delivery to make," the delivery guy spoke.

She placed her hands on her chest and wore a wild smile, "Please tell me the roses are for me... please...," she teased.

He looked at her and then away promptly at the name on the card attached to the flowers, "It depends on whether or not your name is Alice Fallowes."

"Awww no, my name is Kate, sorry," she sighed. "Let me see where she works."

She looked away from him to begin typing the name he mentioned to her into her computer to search the employee database. The delivery man patiently waited while he looked around the office. He caught sight of Poland Air workers working on an air duct, one of the workers walked past him carrying a ladder, he nodded at him. The Poland Air worker nodded back.

———————

The Poland Air worker turned the corner and headed for the bathroom. He stepped in and walked to the back of the bathroom, set up the ladder and climbed up to remove one of the ceiling tiles so he could access the vent above. For a moment, the restroom remained silent, and the room felt empty even with three men in it. Two Ostroff, Kaufman and Fuchs Law firm employees went about their business ignoring the Poland Air worker who tinkered up in the ceiling.

One of the men headed off to use the facilities just as the Poland Air worker stepped back down from the ladder.

Wiping his face clean of sweat, "It is hot as hell up here," the Poland Air worker lamented.

The man by the hand wash basin looked towards the Poland Air worker, "You definitely can say that again."

The other man finishing his business ventured towards the sink to wash his hands, halted and turned around, "When will the damn thing be back up and running again?"

The Poland Air worker interjected, "Well it's hard to tell."

The two lawyers stopped to look at him with raised brows and watched him walk over to his tool box on the sink to open it.

"Every job requires a different tool," he spoke ambiguously.

Without hesitation, he pulled out a nine-millimeter Glock with a suppressor attached to the end of it and pulled the trigger. The first man mercifully didn't know what hit him as he fell to the ground dead. Hearing the commotion, the other man turned to see the bloody crumpled body on the floor. The other man looked up in wide eyed horror just in time to see the gun pointed at him. The last thing he saw was the flash of the muzzle right before he felt the hot lead lodge in between his eyes too. The body fell to the ground in a low thud that brought a smile to the face of the Poland Air worker. He stared at the two lifeless bodies on the floor.

"You should be much cooler now," he said sarcastically.

Sneaking his gun underneath his shirt, he walked to the door slowly and looked around to ascertain if he was being watched.

Exiting, he locked the bathroom door gently and placed an "Out of Order" sign on the handle of the door. He took a good look at his watch expectantly and within a few seconds, a lady walked out of the "Women's Room" just a few feet from him, with a handkerchief she wiped her hands and her gun clean of blood. She slowly locked the door behind her as well and placed an identical "Out of Order" sign on the door.

She looked at him and smiled, "This whole place is going to hell."

With her purse by her side, she walked away and flipped her handgun into her purse before walking in the opposite direction from where he had come.

He watched her disappear into the right before pulling out a radio, "The bathrooms are all aired out."

"Copy!" the voice responded.

Silence followed afterwards.

————————

The delivery man at the reception desk waited for Kate impatiently while she ran the name through the system. He didn't seem interested in her findings anymore, while looking around the floor impatiently.

"I'm sorry but I cannot find her name in the computer," Kate apologized. "Are you certain you have the right office?"

The delivery man nodded positively to show he was certain. While she fiddled with her keyboard in bid to assist him, he pulled out a machine gun from the large box of roses. He looked around and nodded to the others, as they mirrored his actions one at a time they began pulling out automatic weapon from various hiding places and soon all of the Poland Air workers all had munitions by their sides and looks of unrelenting determination on their faces.

Within seconds, they opened fire on the unsuspecting group of people. Chaos and mayhem erupted in the room immediately as people began scurrying around in fear and meeting their death as bullets pierced different parts of their bodies. A chorus of heart gurgling screams and gun fire filled the room, followed by the sounds of glass and furniture being destroyed by the hail of bullets and the bodies that crashed in to them. Suddenly it was over, an eerie macabre silence settled in the room, everyone except the attackers are dead. A man yells out breaking the silence.

"We have four minutes! The press and police have been notified! Green! Get into character and hall ass down stairs." Dale ordered.

Green took some time to look around then ran out of the room. Ostroff, Kaufmam & Fuchs law firm took up the entire fifteenth floor. He busied himself looking for an undamaged computer terminal. Most of them were shot up to hell and nonfunctioning. He smiled as he noticed the sightless eyes of a woman looking at him, a bullet hole placed neatly in her forehead. A clean kill. But what made him smile was the blueish light that was reflected in those lifeless eyes. He walked over to her and Green pushes the body out of the chair. "Sorry my dear." He mockingly whispered as body hits the floor and Green sat down in the chair.

Cracking his knuckles and wearing a smile he quietly whispered to himself, "Let's see what we have here. My name is Bob Dunn, and I just started working at Ostroff, Kaufman and Fuchs Law firm two weeks ago."

Typing into the keyboard he quickly entered all the relevant information. He then back dated what he did and then erased the log information. Green waved over to one of his colleagues and pointed to the computer. Understanding, the other man came over and riddled the computer with bullets until it smoked and caught fire. Satisfied, Green stepped over to relatively clean part of the office where he stripped off his Poland air jump suit.

Underneath his jumpsuit he wore a well-tailored suit, he stuck his hand into the breast pocket of his suit and took out a pair glasses which he gently placed on his face. His look was different now and had an air of professionalism that fit the office atmosphere.

Dale nodded on him to proceed. Green walked out of the room and towards the inner workings of the building, before taking a detour down the stairs, when an incoming soldier stopped him with a raised hand.

"You're not going down like that are you? Here let me help you get in character." the man said.

"I got this Hayes," Green tried assuring him.

Hayes looked at him and pulled out his gun, immediately pointing it at Green and shooting him in his arm first, and then firing another shot into his leg. Green cursed and yelled aloud as the hot feel of the bullets tore into his flesh.

"Fuck! What the hell is wrong with you? Did you have to shoot me twice?" Green groaned and fumed in pain.

He fell to the floor and nursed the injury in agony while Hayes walked away laughing. Green waited a few more minutes before struggling to get to his feet and began limping with his bloody leg as well as holding his wounded arm.

CHAPTER NINETEEN

It didn't take long for the entire melee to get the attention of the authorities, just as the armed men had planned. The blaring sounds of sirens filled the air, followed by the screeching of ambulance sirens. The street was cleared immediately to accommodate rescue and police vehicles. Within minutes, a police barricade was erected just a few feet from the Ostroff, Kaufman & Fuchs building.

The media from various news channels made their presence known, doing their best to provide an exclusive piece on what was going on inside. A medley of reporters all speaking at once sounded like a person speaking in a strange language as their incoherent voices blended together. Their cameramen, to the best of their abilities tried to paint an exclusive picture of the mayhem outside the building. Each media outlet speculated on what might be happening until the official story could be verified.

Joan Cooper had just rushed to the scene. She looked like a crazed lady with her hair barely in place and makeup hastily thrown on. She looked like she had just climbed out of the bed of some football player—like she did back in the day, when she was already 30 minutes late for class. She cursed. It had been five long years of fighting, and sometimes sleeping, her way to the position she had now.

She still had her looks; but in this industry, 30 is considered old. If she was going to get away from the fluff pieces and start doing some real journalism, now was the time. Her supervisor's warning about getting there or it would be her ass on the line didn't steady her confidence. It was the first real piece she would be shooting in a week, and it felt long overdue.

"Are we late?" Joan asked her cameraman, already knowing the answer.

He did his best to shake his head and lie, hoping to give her some false sense of assurance, which she could clearly see past. He had been trying to get into her pants for two months, like he even had a shot. He didn't have anything she needed or wanted. She fixed her hair one more time before pulling down her skirt at its hem, making certain everything was where it was supposed to be. She looked at her blouse and undid one more button, showing a bit more cleavage. At this point, it couldn't hurt. Tomorrow she would go for respectability and finesse. It was always tomorrow, which is why she would never be truly respected in the field. She picked up the microphone and held it to her mouth.

The reporter took a deep breath as the cameraman counted her down from three to one. Joan Cooper closed her eyes at the count of three and opened them on one to begin the show.

"I'm standing outside of Leopold Plaza, home to many of the top money-making companies in the world. Ostroff, Kaufman & Fuchs Law firm is one of the most notable tenants and the latest victim of a violent terrorist attack. This prosperous firm has done work for many film stars, like Blake DeMay Jr., and movie director Devin Constantine, as well as many political figures. A year ago, the firm won $80 million in a civil litigation lawsuit against Iranian nationalist Reched Shirazi. The man is currently serving life in prison for the deaths of 126 people in the bombing of the Rockefeller Concourse and Convention Hub four years ago. About an hour ago, his followers took control of the 15th floor and have proclaimed they will begin executing hostages if the American government doesn't release Reched. They are also demanding a ransom of $24 million. Ostroff, Kaufman & Fuchs has 121 employees working out of the Leopold Plaza facility. Our hopes and prayers are with them and their families.

She waited for the blinking light on the camera to turn off before sighing.

It wasn't her best piece of work. She had been late to the party, so to speak, and now she was paying for it. She needed something different, something the other reporters weren't covering. Most of them were already doing background pieces on Reched's child-hood and upbringing. They also had state-of-the-art equipment in their news vans. Joan's network was way behind the times. She was lucky her cameraman was even shooting in HD. Her van still had VHS tape decks. The only advantage they had, if it could even be categorized as a benefit, was that their file sizes were small enough to cut together pieces and upload them to the station faster than competitors. The one thing Joan was good at was thinking quickly on her feet. She would turn this into a story that covered the victims. She looked at her cameraman, Chris, and called him over.

"Focus your shots on the 15th floor. Try to get some footage of any kind of movement. Hostages would be good, a shot of one of the terrorist would be golden." Chris nodded and got to work.

Joan started to scan the crowd forming on the street. She needed to find someone, anyone, who might be connected to the law firm.

The crowd had been growing for some time now. Standing behind the barriers, people murmured and questioned one another about what was going on inside. Some of the people assembled outside lived in the building, they wanted answers to subside their fears.

"You need to step back, you cannot go past the blockade," a policeman could be heard desperately trying to keep the people in order.

Joan was in the crowd taking names and trying to figure out who she would interview first. She had three good leads as to who would help frame the story she wanted to tell when the troubling sound of heavy-duty vans speeding towards the area caught her attention.

Their presence had been long overdue, considering the hostage situation. The group responsible for the act were well known for their brutality and disregard for human life. It was only a matter of time before the FBI arrived.

While the cops had their hands full, five black vans pulled into the area, stopping at the building entrance. All the eyes in the area were fixated on the vans, as the doors opened and men donning identical black uniforms, heads covered by helmets, began marching out in unison. Holding large crates filled with specialized equipment, they were prepared for the situation at hand. They worked and moved quickly and quietly, showing they had the entire ordeal under control. It didn't take long for those within the building to notice them too. Like clockwork, in response to the FBI team's arrival, a window shattered somewhere on the 15th floor. A masked figure holding an automatic firearm screamed in broken English from within the building. Chris, the cameraman, was the only one with a lens on the action.

"You have refused to meet our demands! You seem to think we are here to joke, so we assume a demonstration will help move your minds," he yelled.

The speaker stood at the window long enough for people to notice him before disappearing again. The sound of gunfire heard from inside was gut-wrenching. The silence afterwards didn't provide comfort. The man returned to the window, this time clutching a woman by her blonde hair.

He made sure all eyes below were on him before tossing the woman out the broken window. She plummeted towards the ground. Watchers gasped, and others clamped their hands over their eyes. The body landed on the ground with a sickening thud for all to hear.

Joan ran over to Chris, feeling a mixture of horror and delight that made her sick to her stomach.

"Did you get that," she asked anxiously.

Chris grinned excitedly. "You bet your ass I did!"

Joan grinned to herself. That shot would cement her career. She might even get a promotion if she worked it right. Chris didn't know it yet, but Joan was going to rock his world tonight.

It was the straw that broke the camel's back. Captain Sidney McBrien was livid. He was tired of these foreigners coming into his country and then complaining about what they encounter. These fuckers killed innocent people. For what? It didn't make any sense. If he had his way, this confrontation would end right here, right now. Not years later, with the government and court system spending millions of dollars on trials to prove guilt.

"That maniac just shot a hostage and threw the body out of the window," he yelled with frustration in his eyes. "I want snipers across the street and on top of every god damn building right now!"

The police officers swiftly did as instructed. The day just got messier, and there was no telling how much more bloodshed to expect.

Captain McBrien watched two men in black suits walk over to him, holding out their badges.

"Captain McBrien, I am special agent David Sherwood, and this is my partner, special agent Leonard Patterson. We are with the FBI Anti-terrorist unit. We need to pick your brain on who is up there and what is going on."

Sherwood's words were more demanding than just a simple ask. This was his crime scene, but they were on the same team, so he updated the agents accordingly.

"Yeah, the situation is that one of those psychopaths just shot and killed and innocent civilian and dumped the body out the window, just in time for the fucking six o'clock news!"

The men looked in the direction of his hand while he continued.

With a sigh and a show of exasperation, the Captain continued. "I have men who have been on the force for over 20 years who are puking their guts out after seeing that poor woman's body splattered across the pavement."

Agent Patterson turned back to look at Captain McBrien. "In these kinds of situations, the terrorists usually send a hostage with a list of their demands. Has that happened yet?"

"Yeah, the nut job sent down a list with one of the hostages, but not before he shot the guy in the arm and leg," Captain McBrien confirmed.

Patterson looked at his partner briefly. "What happened to the guy?"

"He's over there in the ambulance. You better hurry, they are about to take that guy to the hospital to treat him," Captain McBrien suggested.

The men made an attempt to leave before Sherwood turned back around.

"Did they make mention of who they are?" he asked.

The Captain shook his head. "No, just the usually garbage! They are asking for twenty million, plus the release of their leader."

The sound of his words made the men jolt back to his attention.

"And their leader is?" Patterson asked this time.

Captain McBrien tucked his hands into his pocket before responding. "His name sounded something like...umm, that Arab guy who blew up Rockefeller a couple of years back."

He watched the two agents' eyes widen immediately as they felt their insides cringe.

"Reched Shirazi," Patterson inquired.

"Yeah, that's the guy."

Sherwood shook his head fervently; kicking against a harmless can in his path.

He turned to Captain McBrien. "Captain McBrien, as of this moment, and here on out, this entire situation is now under the jurisdiction of the FBI."

The Captain had seen it coming. The local police were definitely out of their league. This thing has gotten political. All he could hope for is that it ended with bullets in the head of these terrorists and the death penalty for Reched.

"Leonard go see that hostage now," Sherwood ordered.

Captain McBrien growled. "That suits me just fine. Just get that son of a bitch!"

The ambulance slowly started to move, with its lights flashing. Patterson had to run as fast as his legs could carry him to stop the ambulance from leaving. He was able to jump in front of the vehicle, causing it to lurch to a stop. The ambulance driver blared his siren to get Leonard to move out of the way. Patterson slapped the hood a couple of times then yelled at the driver. "FBI! Open up! I need to talk to the guy in the back!" He held his ID and badge high enough for the driver to see.

He walked towards the back of the ambulance and knocked on the door, waiting for a response. The veins around his neck throbbed as he caught his breath.

The ambulance's back doors finally swung open to reveal two perplexed looking EMTs. He cleared his throat, holding out his badge as he spoke.

"FBI! I need to speak with that man, it's a matter of national security."

The lady shared a brief glance with her colleague, pointing to the man behind her. "He is right there, but he has lost a lot of blood and needs to be taken to the ER as soon as possible. He is in stable condition for now."

Patterson stepped into the ambulance and walked over to the patient, who looked like he had seen hell. His wounded arm looked bad.

He leaned closer to the man to whisper into his ear. "Hi, how are you doing?"

The question sounded stupid, but it needed to be said.

"My name is Special Agent Leonard Patterson with the FBI. What is your name," he asked?

The man strained his voice as he managed to respond. "Bob Dunn."

His voice sounded cracked, barely making its way out of his mouth as he tried hard not to overly exert himself.

"Looks like you had a busy day, Bob," Patterson tried to sound as sympathetic as possible." Do you want to tell me about it?"

"They came out of nowhere," he began.

Patterson listened attentively, but there was something wrong with the way Bob looked at him. Something wasn't quite right, but he couldn't put his finger on it.

"We didn't resist, but they beat us for no good reason. I watched them take turns beating Diane. I think they just enjoyed hearing her scream. One guy ripped her shirt open and started fondling her breast. I thought they were going to rape her and I snapped! I couldn't take it anymore," he coughed. "I ran over and shoved one of them off of her and then they…Oh God!"

Bob burst into tears like a child. Patterson did his best to console the man, but there was that feeling again. Something was gnawing at him. Something was off.

"It is okay, what happened," Patterson pushed on.

"They shot her…they killed her, and…and there was nothing I could do but watch. It was all my fault!"

"In most scenarios like the one you were in, it is hardly anyone's fault," Agent Patterson said in a soft tone. "You have to believe that. Now we want to help the rest of those people who are still there. Can you tell me what else happened?"

"They laughed at me while I ran, and then I heard the gunshots. One struck me in the arm."

"What happened next Bob? What happened and what can you tell me?" Patterson asked.

Bob sighed and opened his eyes to look at the federal agent.

"I hit the ground and grabbed my arm in pain. Then they started to speak in Arabic, I think. A couple of minutes later, one of the men said "Come here hero! We have a job for you!" "They gave me the videotape and told me to get out. When I hesitated, they shot me in the leg."

The agent took the time to think as he pulled out a notepad from the pocket beneath his jacket. He scribbled down some words, which Bob could not see, before looking back up with his pen in hand.

"Can you tell me how many terrorists you think are in there?"

"Somewhere near twenty I think," Bob replied.

"Thanks a lot Bob. Everything will be alright from here, and I am very sure these guys will take good care of you," Agent Leonard said, concluding the conversation.

Bob managed to smile and watched as Patterson tell the EMTs to head off to the hospital. He must be getting cynical, Paterson thought to himself for being so suspicious of Bob. He pushed the thought out of his mind and made his way back to his partner, who stood in front of a black van and speaking with Captain McBrien and a few other agents.

"The terrorists sent over a videotape with the hostage after they let him go," Patterson informed the group.

Agent Sherwood turned to the Captain, with a wry look across his face and a slight frown on his forehead. "Where is the videotape, Captain? How come we weren't shown this evidence earlier?" Sherwood barked accusingly.

The Captain pointed to his car and led them over. "We have it right here in the car and I was hoping on turning it over soon."

"Have you guys watched it," Sherwood asked the cops who ac-companied them to the car.

"Are you kidding? Half of these young bucks didn't even know what it was. Who the hell uses videotapes anymore?"

The word rang out like a church bell on Sunday morning. Did Joan hear them right, as the entourage of officers walked by their news van. She ran behind them yelling, hoping to get their attention.

"Officer? Captain!" Joan yelled out. The group turned around to face her. "Did I hear you correctly? You have a videotape of the terrorist demands?"

Annoyed, Captain McBrien cut her off. "Look miss, we don't have time to give you a statement or comment!"

Joan pressed her advantage. "Our news van has a tape player! We just need a moment to hook it up."

"Who uses those things anymore," the Captain said sardonically.

"No one," Joan replied. "It is an old van with mostly obsolete equipment, but it gets the job done."

It was then Joan noticed the federal agents. The reporter began to pepper them immediately with endless questions.

"What exactly do these terrorists want? Do they want more money? Do you think they may have killed any more hostages?"

If there was anything Agent Patterson despised, it was press.

"We will inform you of the situation once we can establish what's going on. Now, please let us do our job. Thank you."

Agents Sherwood and Patterson walked past the pesky reporter and over to the cameraman in the van. Sherwood tapped on the van's body to alert Chris of their presence. Chris immediately took off the headset and looked at them with wary eyes. Joan followed them but kept her distance.

"Hey, you," Agent David called out. "Can you play this thing for us?"

He extended his arm with the videotape in it and handed it to Chris.

"Yeah sure, let me warm up this baby for you," Chris replied.

As Chris turned around to prepare his VCR to play the tape, Joan signaled to him, in hopes none of the agents could see her.

"Make a copy," she mouthed.

He nodded at her, he discreetly hit the "record" button on one of the VCR's and inserted the videotape in a different VCR positioned above the other machine and pressed play.

Agents Sherwood and Patterson moved closer to the screen. The image of a man dressed in desert camouflage, with a cowl covering his face, appeared on the monitor. The man on the recording began speaking.

"My name is Sudir Pascaru. By the time you see this, we will have taken control of the Ostroff, Kaufman & Fuchs law firm. We will have taken the people hostage to pay for the crimes against my people and our leader, Reched Shirazi. Our demands are that the Americans release Reched Shirazi. We also demand $24 million for the wrongful deaths of 1,345 of my people during the endless war you wage. Along with this sum, the President will admit publicly that the action taken against my country is unlawful.

If our demands are not met, we will kill everyone and the whole world will see as it happens. Either in blood! Or money! You capitalist pigs will pay!"

His words echoed as he spoke.

The tape finally came to an end and snow appeared on the monitor. Chris gave Joan a wink, which made her smile. When all was said and done, she might even win an Emmy.

"What do we do now," McBrien asked while scratching his head.

Sherwood looked lost momentarily before finally speaking. "We need to attack, and we need to do it now!"

"Leonard, get the Anti-Terrorist Unit ready and raring to go now," he yelled.

McBrien looked lost.

"What is going on," he managed to ask.

Sherwood gave no response initially before speaking. "I don't trust these people to keep their word. I've seen this before! They are going to kill everyone in there, and I will be damned if I let that happen on my watch."

Patterson ran off immediately to begin barking out orders to the unit already assembled.

"Sweet mother of God!" McBrien muttered.

––––––––––

The malevolent plan became real. In order for this to work, there could be no survivors. There could be no doubt as to what had happened today.

The "Poland Air" clothing had been thrown in a pile on the floor.

All gunmen who massacred the employees of Ostroff, Kaufman & Fuchs law firm now wore fitting black business suits. One man poured a liquid on the pile of "Poland Air" uniforms and lit a match dropping it on the pile. The fabric burst into flames. Dale had just gotten through donning his business suit with when he turned to the group to speak.

 "The FBI will be up here in two minutes, and we need to prep the room as planned and be ready to move!" Dale ordered.

The men set about to enact their plan, first smearing their suits in dirt and blood from large containers they had brought with them.

Dale's men then opened large body bags with unconscious members of the Black Dagger. They placed the bodies strategically around the room. In the hands of the unconscious men, they placed Mac-10 machine guns.

Dale then placed two devices in the room. The first device sprayed an aerosol mist of smelling salts into the air. The other device was connected to a remote detonator attached to eighty pounds of C4 explosive. The aerosol mist that now permeated the air started to wake up the Black Dagger terrorists out of their comatose state. Dale yelled in Arabic, "Amrikiin! Amrikiin!"

Instinctively, the terrorists from the Black Dagger started shooting wildly in all directions. Dale's men prepared for this situation already had their guns aimed at the Black Dagger easily picked them off one by one until they were all dead.

Dale made certain to inspect everything as it happened while looking at his watch to make sure they were making good time. He raised his hand and began to count down. "5...4...3...2..."

"I... Now," he screamed with all his might.

Within seconds, his men ran out of the area and down the stairs. Dale pulled the trigger on the detonation device and the entire 15th floor exploded in fireball.

Dale inspected the stairwell once again before ordering his men to begin phase two of the plan.

————————

Special Agent David Sherwood and Agent Leonard Patterson had just shared a brief conversation when the eruption came tearing through the air from above. They looked up immediately, fearing the worst. They glanced up just in time to see the inferno blow out all the windows on the 15th floor.

"Shit! We are too late!" Agent Sherwood screeched. "We need to get our team up there now!"

With a wave of his hand, Patterson gave the Anti-Terrorist Unit orders to storm the building. All rushed towards the door with their heads lowered, every person scattering to a pre-determined direction. Some headed for the front door, while others stormed the side of the building, progressing through the service entry doors.

They got into the building and made their way in until they reached the 15th floor. They took a long pause before swiftly moving towards the offices of Ostroff, Kaufman & Fuchs.

Alan, the man in command, pulled off his helmet and balaclava and looked around the room before speaking. "Secure the room!"

The men scurried around checking each room. One officer circled around until he was standing in front of Alan and spoke. "It looks like we are too late, sir!"

"Christ! What the hell is this meant to prove? God have mercy on us all," Alan exclaimed while taking out his radio. He spoke into it slowly. "You had better get up here, Sir."

Agent Patterson held the radio in his hand. Alan's voice cracked over the radio with a hiss of static behind it. "It's a bloody mess up her sir."

"God damn it," Agent Patterson swore. "Get these people back!"

Dale and his men slipped out of an alley near the building and disappeared into the large crowd gathered there.

CHAPTER TWENTY

The one thing lacking in the desert, in the middle of nowhere, was information from the outside world. Reading the paper while enjoying a cup of coffee was the one thing that Zachary missed in the morning. Now he was fiddling with the radio in the hopes of tuning in a local station.

The sound of radio static filled the room. Ralph tried to focus on the task at hand—comparing the time-lapse photos with his drawings of the temple's interiors—but the noise filling the air was a bit distracting.

Ralph looked over to Zachary, the man's persistence to find a signal on that thirty-year-old radio was starting to bug him.

"You know, you're never going to tune into any station from all the way out, here," Ralph informed him. "The bandwidth isn't strong enough."

"Sometimes early in the morning I can tune into the local news station," Zachary said while still fiddling with the knobs on the radio. "A lot is happening out there in the world."

Ralph raised an eyebrow in curiosity.

"Things are happening out there. Bad things. I need to find out what they are," Zachary said with a sigh.

Ralph acknowledged his worries with the nod. He had thought often about what was happening out in the world but then decided there was nothing he could do and just focus on his work.

"We will be back there in the world soon enough," Ralph declared.

"Speaking of which, I was wondering when we were shipping out?"

Zachary took his attention away from the radio and eased back into his chair to think. He looked out the tent flap and contemplated the situation before closing his eyes and sighing.

"It depends on our two friends down there and how much progress they have been able to make," Zachary finally spoke.

So much depended on what they are be able to decipher. He knew once their discovery was made public, an inevitable legal battle over who owns the archaeological artifacts would ensue.

The scrolls alone were priceless, and they had found so much more than that.

Zachary had spent almost a million dollars of his own money on this project. The grant the university had given them was gone, too. In total, two-and-a-half-million dollars. Damn Steven Spielberg and his Indiana Jones movies. There was a time when Zachary would have been able to sell the artifacts to the museum willing to pay the most. He never considered himself a treasure hunter, but nowadays even the attempt to sell an artifact to anyone is frowned upon.

He was hoping for partage, under partage, Zachary's team had provided the expertise and materials for the excavations. The local government would then share whatever was found. Half of what was discovered would go to the local government's archaeological museums the other half to the Ludlow Russell University the entity that employed Zachary's team.

It was through this system that Harvard and Yale built up their collections to create their archaeological museums and Ludlow Russell University would do the same.

He doubted the university would pay him anymore money, He would be content to just walk away with the knowledge, using it for speaking engagements and book deals, that was the new path to fame and fortune nowadays. A laugh from Ralph brought Zachary back to the present.

"If those two have their way, I think they might choose to stay down there forever," Ralph scoffed.

He wasn't joking, and Zachary didn't see it as one either.

"What makes you say that?" Zachary questioned.

Ralph abandoned what he was doing to explain. "Well, two nights ago, when I got through with my work down there, I figured I'd go check up on them both to see if they were okay."

Zachary nodded.

"When I got to the fourth room, I found the two of them laughing as if nothing else mattered. They seemed very relaxed with each other," he explained.

The statement brought a smug look from Zachary.

"It sounds like your jealous," he said.

Ralph managed to smile. "Maybe a little. Who would ever think a bookworm like him and a woman like Reena would hit it off."

Zachary nodded in acknowledgement. However, stranger things have been known to happen.

"So, what were they laughing about," he asked Ralph.

Ralph shrugged. "That's just it. I don't know. I couldn't understand them."

Zachary was just about to ask Ralph what he was talking about when the static from the radio cleared and a low voice could be heard breaking through the white noise. He fondled with the radio's knob until the station was almost crystal clear. A female voice broke the silence and connected them to the outside world.

Renegades from The Black Dagger terrorist group took over an American law firm last night, killing everyone inside and then themselves. A note left behind stated that this is just the beginning. This is Nirmala Moisa, WWN. In other news, rumors still persist that two American scientists have somehow been able to safely enter Devil's Fork, straining relations between the USA and other countries.

Zachary turned to look at Ralph, both men shocked by the latest news.

CHAPTER TWENTY-ONE

As Roland immersed himself in the magic, he became aware of something so complex and yet so very basic that the very thought of it nearly blew his mind.

Everything is connected. The idea itself seemed like nonsense, like a line from a Star Wars movie. Yet, as he worked the magic in his head, there it was.

There was also a deeper level to it, he had almost missed it. Not only is everything connected, but the possibilities of anything and everything are infinite.

This new idea horrified him and fascinated him all at the same time. He started to shake. Thankfully, a frustrated cry from Reena brought him back to himself.

The strange language still gave Reena difficulty, she was trying her best to pronounce the words properly. It surprised her how quickly she had picked it up. It felt so natural to speak, almost as if she had been speaking in this language all her life. Yet, like striking a wrong chord on a guitar, she knew instinctively when her pronunciations were off. Roland's phrasing and dialect, on the other hand, was perfect.

"What am I getting wrong?" Reena conceded.

He chuckled briefly before answering. ""You are doing just fine. You're just nervous. Take your time pronouncing the words."

Reena stared at him and smiled before taking a deep breath and trying hard to speak again.

"Hei sado key bena," she attempted.

As she spoke, Reena traced the symbols in the air, just like Roland had taught her. Roland tried not to react as his synesthesia kicked in. He immediately saw her mistake, as her words took on a dark, muddy color. It was like he had perfect pitch; her words were slightly off. Even if he wanted too, he couldn't really explain to her what she did wrong, she would just have to practice.

A flame appeared in front of them for a brief moment, then fizzed out.

Reena screamed in frustration. "I can't do this!"

"I know it might seem difficult, but if there is anyone here who will understand it fluently, then it is you, Reena."

Reena closed her eyes, imagining the words in her mind, letting them flow out like a cool breeze escaping past her lips. Roland silently mimicked her words with his mouth, she was so close to getting it right, the colors of her words appeared in front of him.

"Keep on with it Reena...remain steady and concentrate."

A flame flickered in front of them again briefly before burning out.

Reena looked around the room, searching for an object to unleash her frustration on. She settled for a pile of rocks, kicking the mound and watching the stones scatter.

"Well it's just another stupid light spell. I can create the light sphere, why do I have to know this one as well?"

Roland moved closer and placed his hand on her left shoulder.

"Everything is connected. I'm learning right along with you. If you know this part and connect it with something else, you create something completely different! It is like playing with LEGOs. The small pieces by themselves don't look like much. However, when you start putting those pieces together, you can build anything!"

He hoped his enthusiasm would rub off on her.

"You need to look at it this way," Roland continued by leading her to the chair in the room. "Do you remember the symbol for love? It's the two interlocking symbols. Without one, the other symbol means something completely different. So, my point is, if you know one part and connect with something else…"

Reena watched him stare into nothing. She slowly began to realize what Roland had meant when he said you had to feel it as well. He suddenly looked radiant. His whole body seem to transform. He was almost unrecognizable in this state.

"Hei sado key bena caelatol," Roland whispered.

Although speaking at a whisper, Roland's words bounced off the chamber walls. With his right hand, he traced a symbol in the air and a fireball appeared bright and ominous before them. Reena backed away from the heat. Roland then waved his right hand back and forth; the fireball mimicked his movements. With a sharp wave of his hand towards the wall, the fireball took off flying in that direction before hitting the wall and exploding, illuminating the room in a spark of light.

"Wow," Reena exclaimed.

She took a few seconds to think about what she had seen, and it dawned on her that she had never seen that spell before.

She turned to look at Roland. "Where did you see that particular spell? I didn't see it in the books."

Roland chuckled slightly before speaking. "You will not find it in any book. I kind of made it up."

"You have made this a part of you. How is that possible for you to do it and I cannot," she asked in a bewildered tone.

"You too can do what I do. Reena. You just have to believe you can."

"What does your imagination tell you?" Reena asked.

Roland shrugged and responded. "Everything."

Reena sat down at the table.

She looked back at the intelligent man and duly acknowledged that his level of understanding was way beyond her own. "Are you telling me that there are no limits to what we can do?"

"As far as I can tell, none."

The mere thought of what he said both excited and troubled Reena. There had to be limits, there just had to be a ceiling to keep them in check.

"Something is troubling you," Roland asked after seeing the unsettled look on her face. "You can tell me whatever it is."

"I'm afraid Roland. I'm afraid of other people finding out what we know. This kind of power, in the wrong hands, could be disastrous."

Roland did echo her fears. He had the power of the ancient gods.

The power to create and destroy. Worse than that, he had the power to manipulate and control anyone less powerful. He knew, eventually, he would have the power to take over the world if he wished. That wasn't in his nature. He didn't care for such things. Maybe that's why fate brought him here.

"I felt the same way you do," Roland confessed. "But I believe that I was meant to be here and that you were, too."

He sounded convinced, so sure of himself. The guilt had been eating away at Reena for some time. He has always been so open and patient with her. It was about time she returned the favor. Reena walked towards the entrance and checked the surrounding rooms to be certain they were still the only ones in the temple.

"There is something I have to tell you, Roland, but you must promise to hear me out," she spoke from the door.

Roland looked baffled but agreed.

"Is everything okay? Is something wrong?" Roland sounded anxious.

She shook her head before sitting down.

"We all had our reasons for being here. Before we sent for you. Zachary and Susan came here first. Zachary does believe that the world is going to end but his ultimate goal is," she spoke softly, working out what she wanted to say.

"To make money," Roland offered.

"Yes."

"I know," Roland uttered." "Let's face it, that's what brought us all here initially, right?"

It's true. That was the main motivation for everyone involved. Fortune and glory.

"It might be true for everyone except me," she replied.

Roland was a little bit thrown by her response. "Why are you here then?"

She leaned back into the chair and stared at him for a while.

"I knew what he found was old. I came here hoping to find," she paused.

Roland waited patiently for her to continue.

He moved his chair closer to her, unable to meet her gaze. He repeated to himself in Latin, so softly that she didn't hear him.

"Bene, bene, bene," he murmured. The words translated to "be well."

Her lips were trembling, but she managed to force it out.

"You have been so kind to me Roland," she sobbed. "That means a lot to me. More than you will ever know. I tend not to trust anyone. I've been hurt in the past. I put up these walls around me. I had a child, Roland. A little boy, and he meant more to me than life itself. He died...because of me. I'm sick and will die unless a cure is found. Do you understand what I'm telling you?"

Roland felt the air get rather uncomfortable between them. He had never seen Reena get this emotional and it felt strange. He was good at mimicking an emotional response, but he rarely felt them. When he did, he wasn't sure what to do.

He watched her bow her head closer to the table, letting the hot rolls of tears run down her face. Roland awkwardly hugged her. The gesture was clumsy, but Reena didn't seem to notice.

"What sickness is it," he managed to inquire.

"Hunter virus number six," she replied through her tears. "Now you understand why I need to find that cure and why I am here. It has nothing to do with the money."

He finally understood why she stayed awake for the majority of the night, too scared to sleep. Why she constantly drank coffee and took those pills. It also explained her strange mood swings. Like tumblers falling into place, it all made sense to him now. Besides finding the cure, the work they did was an escape mechanism for her, taking her mind off the disease so she wouldn't fall sleep as much and wake up screaming from nightmares—an occurrence that happened frequently. He knew about the disease all too well and what it could do. It starts with sudden weight loss. As the disease progresses, you suffer from memory loss, paranoia, narcolepsy and then death.

"One day you go to sleep and never wake up again," Roland muttered.

Roland sighed and closed his eyes momentarily before opening them again. He rubbed his temple hard and tried to think, while it felt hard and almost impossible to gather his thoughts into place.

"What are you thinking about?" she asked.

Roland looked at her with a thin smile. "What was your son's name?"

"Demetrios," she replied.

"Nice name, Reena. We have both been through a lot these past couple of months. I will do everything within my power to find you a cure."

She looked into his eyes. "Do you really think we could find a cure?"

"If I can't, I know that they can," he said while stretching his hands around the room.

"Who?" she asked, frantically examining the room.

"Our friends encased in the crystal," he responded.

Reena looked at him in disbelief.

"Are you trying to tell me you can bring them all back from the dead?" she asked in amazement.

"No. I'm telling you that they are not dead."

She looked startled and her jaw dropped.

"When do we do it?" she looked on in expectation.

"We can do it as soon as you are ready," Roland confirmed.

For the first time in a long time she felt hopeful. Filled with a new confidence, Reena was reinvigorated with a strength that filled her entire being as she leapt from her seat.

She looked around, then stared into the air, tracing symbols with her finger. She felt the spell take over.

She passionately vocalized the words "Hei sado key bena caelato!"

A fireball appeared bright and ominous before them. Reena then waved her right hand towards the wall; the fireball took off flying before hitting the wall and exploding. It happened exactly like Roland had done it before.

Roland was impressed with her progress.

She smiled and leapt into his arms. The sudden move startled Roland, but he didn't pull away. In fact, he eased into the hug. For the first time in a long time, he felt something he thought had escaped him long ago, affection. He let himself enjoy the moment.

CHAPTER TWENTY-TWO

What is the definition of destiny? The thought buzzed around in Keith's head like an insect as he walked through the gardens with Diaona.

Is it really something you cannot change? Keith tried to wrap his mind around the concept. He tried to figure out exactly what had happened to him.

He shouldn't feel so comfortable around this woman. Is she a woman? She has wings! The thought still filled him with awe, and yet, here he was, clinging to her every word.

More than once, he caught himself taking in the aroma of her hair, which smelled like honeysuckle. He looked at her body with a longing he couldn't put into words. When he looked in her eyes, he lost himself in a world without boundaries.

Is this what a soulmate is?

Keith was so lost in his thoughts that he forgot Michael and Zar were walking ahead of them. When he looked at Diaona, he blushed. She blushed back. Can she read his thoughts?

"How old are you," Keith inquired.

"I am just entering my tenth cycle," Diaona replied immediately.

Keith realized he had no idea what a cycle was, prompting him to ask for clarity.

"What would that equate to in human years?"

She took her time to think it through before responding.

"I think in your human years I will be 491 years old."

Keith gasped immediately, unable to believe his ears.

"Wow! You look fantastic!"

"How old are you?" Diaona asked with a smile.

Keith grinned. "Thirty-eight."

"Well, if it will put your mind at ease, we are about the same age emotionally and spiritually."

Keith considered her words.

He couldn't stop looking at Diaona, the attraction was so strong it was almost overwhelming. Was she flirting with him? Keith couldn't tell, he just knew he wanted to spend as much time with her as possible.

"I can recall things, remember things I have yet to experience," Keith explained.

"It's the power of the birth crystal. It will eventually, if you allow it, guide you to your one," Diaona confessed.

"My life-mate."

Michael and Zar were a few paces ahead, talking about the world above. Although Michael was only half listening. He wasn't sure what to do. The longer they stayed in this world, the less sense it made to him. Michael turned back to look at Keith, deeply engrossed in a conversation with Diaona. Were they flirting with each other? Michael immediately though about the complications. How does interspecies dating work? He didn't believe they were gods anymore, perhaps a different race of humans. They could never be together. She has wings for Christ sake. Michael felt ashamed of his thoughts. He sounded like a bigot and a racist. His brain was a jumbled mess, filled with things he didn't understand. Zar said something to Michael that brought him back to the here and now.

"What is this science you keep speaking of," Zar questioned.

Michael was glad to occupy his mind with something he did know.

When Keith was a young boy he asked his mother how she knew his father was the one she was going to marry. At the time the answer seemed silly and farfetched. She said she just knew. Oddly enough, Keith began to understand the answer as he looked at Diaona.

Keith continued his conversation with Diaona. "Was I right?"

"Yes," she responded. "Exactly right."

"How did I even know that,"' Keith asked in a startled tone.

"You must have an old mind," she responded. "It is one very few people possess."

"What do you mean by an old mind?" he asked.

Zar took an interest in Keith's conversation and allowed him and Diaona to catch up to him. He smiled and answered Keith's question.

"It means you are special, Keith. You are a rare soul. You are connected to someone who is not a humanidauns," he explained.

"I'm still not sure what you mean," Keith confessed.

Zar replied immediately. "You must be a mixed breed of some kind."

Keith gasped, a mixed breed? What exactly did Zar mean? He wasn't an animal, a mongrel. Humans are above mere animals, and yet if he followed the laws of science, he knew that he was indeed an animal. The only other choices he had, according to his fifth-grade teacher, Mr. Moran, were vegetable and mineral. He didn't mean to get angry. Diaona saw his discomfort.

"Like a dog of a different origin," Keith asked in a rather annoyed tone.

"I don't understand what you mean my friend," Zar replied.

Michael answered in an attempt to diffuse the situation.

"It's the word breed, we use that word when talking about, animals lower than us."

Zar smiled sympathetically.

"There are no creatures below or above us. We are all equal in the eyes of the great one. I simply meant that Keith may have come into being from the joining of two different cultures.

Michael suddenly understood Zar.

"You're talking about miscegenation. Are you saying Keith is one of you?"

The word, like many of the words Keith and Michael used, were foreign to Zar. He understood enough, however, to answer Michael's question.

Zar didn't give an immediate response and looked at Diaona first before speaking. "If not one of us, another race other than humanidauns."

Keith let the words fill his ears., taking in deep, slow breaths before speaking.

"I don't know what to say or how to feel," he confessed.

Diaona walked closer to him, putting her hand on to his shoulder. "In time it will all come to you."

Her words didn't entirely reassure him, but they did help him relax. His mind swam with thoughts, desperately shifting as the group strolled ahead.

CHAPTER TWENTY-THREE

They all walked silently down the path, absorbed in their own thoughts. The path widened to reveal a beautiful stone structure. It almost seemed to hum and vibrate as they got closer. Zar walked a few feet in front of the group. He turned to face them, causing them to stop."

"This is the Star Chamber. It was here we were foretold of your arrival."

"You knew we were coming," Michael said in a skeptical tone.

Zar extended his hand towards the door. "Let me show you."

Michael, Keith and Diaona walked behind Zar as he led the way into the temple. Zar whispered something and turned back to look at them with a stern gaze.

"From this point on, I must insist that you take off the wrappings on your feet and bow your heads."

Michael and Keith nodded and began taking off their footwear. Diaona was already barefoot and waited patiently for the two men. Zar inspected them both, and with a look of satisfaction allowed them to proceed.

Michael, who was walking right behind Zar, entered first. He looked around in amazement. Keith and Diaona followed. There was an undeniable feeling of peace and acceptance that washed over them. Similar to the sensation one feels after stepping from the heat into an air-conditioned room during the summer. Michael looked around the structure, whispering to Keith directly behind him.

"This is what I saw in the village. It is almost an identical temple," he murmured.

"Do you feel that," Keith asked.

"What?" Michael inquired, barely able to hear his friend.

Keith snapped at him in a hushed tone. "Quiet, Michael! Listen and feel."

It was obvious Michael had not taken in the whole chamber, as what he saw next perplexed and astonished him.

The Star Chamber was round with a dome ceiling. Floating from its center was a star-shaped crystal.

It glowed with a pale blue light. Four nine-foot-tall cathedral windows, each set with blue opal, surrounded the room.

The columns separating the windows stretched from the ceiling to the floor. Displayed in the center of the chamber was an ornate gold altar.

On top of the altar, an acacia bush in full bloom sat in a golden planter. The bush was on fire, but the leaves and branches did not burn. Blue light rained down from above, while the altar also seemed to give off its own golden light. Five beautiful, winged women stood in a circle humming a wordless song. Their arms and wings are stretched towards the altar. Keith stared with sacred appreciation.

Michael looked over at Diaona, who seemed to be experiencing the same elation Keith was feeling. He didn't know what was happening or what to think. As if reading and sensing his thoughts, Diaona spoke to Michael.

"Yes Michael, feel the power of Yahweh within and around you," Diaona encouraged.

Michael looked startled. "Yahweh?"

Keith nodded. "God. Don't you feel the power of God in this room, Mike?"

Michael realized he was the only one in the room not in a euphoric state. What the hell was going on? Yes, this was all very impressive, and he had to admit the burning bush was a nice touch, but it had to be some kind of illusion. Michael knew that there had to be some kind of scientific explanation. There was a feeling slowly filling him. It spread like a heat that started in his chest and then shot out in all directions. It made the hairs on the back of his neck stand up. Was he light-headed or getting sick? He wondered as he looked to Zar for help.

Zar began praying in his own language. The words didn't sound like the dialect the villagers spoke. It was melodic and light and crawled on his brain like a thousand little spiders. It felt like he could almost understand the strange language, but it was just beyond his reach.

"Mighty Yahweh. You who are all-powerful and all-knowing, we pray to you almighty father! Hear our prayer!"

"We wait of the days of peace to come when we shall live in harmony!" Keith responded to the prayer a surprising tone.

Michael was beyond shocked. Keith responded in the same strange language. Zar, Diaona and Keith all fell to their knees and surrounded the altar with the burning bush. Michael takes a step back as Diaona responds to Keith.

"We who are your humble servants," Diaona implored.

Michael's breathing became shallow, with his heart beating fast in his chest. He immediately broke out in a sweat. Was he having a panic attack? He felt like he couldn't control his body. He looked from Zar to Keith to Diaona. He wanted to cry out for help, but he couldn't talk. He fell on to the cool stone floor, unable to move, when he suddenly hears a voice from within.

"Michael," the voice said.

Michael tried to answer but couldn't. It was so dark all around him and he was truly afraid. The voice called out to him again.

"Michael do not be afraid."

Michael cried out, or at least he thought he did. "Who are you!"

"You know who I am, you have always known. You do not have to believe in me because I already believe in you."

Michael wept. He felt the tears run down his face. His sight returned. He was still surrounded in utter darkness, but he saw a light way off in the distance. It seemed to be miles away. As he stared at the light, it began to grow larger. It was so silent and still in the black void. Michael could not tell if the light moved towards him or if he moved towards the light. The light seemed to be moving and changing color. It flickered from orange to blue. Michael could almost see it. The light was coming from a flame.

As soon as Michael realized this, the room erupted with light. He was back in the Star Chamber with Keith, Diaona and Zar. The light he saw, the one he was focused on, was the burning bush. He was flooded with an overwhelming feeling of love and tranquility.

He listened to them pray and instantaneously realized he could understand them. Did they switch to English just for his benefit he thought? No, the rhythm of their words was different. They were speaking in another language, but Michael could still understand.

Zar clamped his hands together and spoke. "This is the fifth sign of Sibtala and we await one more."

Diaona joined in. "As it was in the beginning."

Keith ended the sentence. "And it will be again."

Diaona, Keith and Zar spoke in unison next. "One with Our Father...one with each other!"

They slowly got up from their knees and began walking towards the south side of the temple where a large door stood. Michael had not realized he was kneeling until he got up. They walked into a dark room. Zar stopped and looked around at the three behind him before speaking.

"Trerealine," he exclaimed.

Standing in the void of darkness, Michael thought he might have another episode but was calmed as he heard the others around him breathing.

Specks of lights appeared, one by one, all around them. At first, it was just a couple of dozen, then hundreds of dots slowly filling the room. It became clear to Michael they were standing in a miniature universe. The dots were stars, or at least the representation of stars. It was by far the most incredible 3D display ever created.

Dumbfounded, Michael addressed Zar. "What is this? I mean, what exactly is going on in here?"

"This is our home and here is where we live," Zar replied while pointing to the third planet from the sun in the simulated miniature universe.

"That's Earth. Why are you showing us this," he asked?

Keith spoke up and provided the answer.

"The quake wasn't an accident, Mike."

Michael didn't know what to say or how to react to the news. He just stared at Keith. Keith smiled and continued.

"Remember the celestial event ten years ago? When all the planets in the solar system became one? It is not unusual for some of the planets to join together, but when all of the planets are one it is a rare event."

Michael frowned before raising an eyebrow. "What do you mean they became one? Wait! You're talking about Alignment Day? When all the planets line up in our solar system? That kind of event only happens every five hundred years!"

Diaona decided to cut in. "Yes Michael, everything became one and all the worlds looked exactly like this."

She waved her hand through the air. The planets danced and moved, lining up behind one another into a straight line. She took a step back for Michael to examine the beauty of what she had created. He reached his hand towards Venus before stopping to admire the entire setup once again.

"This was what opened the seal and led you into our world. In doing so, fulfilling the second sign," she explained.

Of course, it made sense. If the moon has an impact on the Earth, what would happen if all the planets in the solar system came into alignment? Many scientists theorized there would be no real change, but what if they were wrong? Michael felt like his head was being messed with. He wondered if he back-dated the last couple of celestial events would they explain the disappearance of Atlantis? Would the major devastating occurrences in Earth's history coincide with the celestial phenomenon?

Zar spoke matter-of-factly. "It was that event that opened the seal and lead you to our world fulfilling the second sign."

He had heard just too many things and wasn't even sure he could keep up.

"Wait, slow down. Your losing me, how does Keith know so much?" He asked Zar but turned to look at the man who followed him on this expedition into Devil's Fork. Somehow Keith had changed. He seemed wiser.

Keith moved closer to his friend. "Michael, for once in my life, I understand. It is so hard to explain to you."

Michael nodded and listened intently.

"Things like déjà vu and out-of-body experiences, in reality, those are memories from the past," Keith began. "The memories are of who we are and were, and what will become of us later."

Michael felt skeptical but remained patient as he listened.

"Life is a series of stages. We became so scattered over the centuries that only fragments remained," Keith did his best to keep things simple. "I want you to imagine all the different religions in the world. Do you think that it's a coincidence that Islam, Judaism and Christianity all follow the same principles? Imagine all the different religions in the world being one, and it will all come to make sense to you."

Michael could see some reason in it.

"What does this mean for us? What does it mean for our world," he asked.

Zar took over the conversation by answering Keith's question.

"It is the six signs of Sibtala. So, it was written. From the beginning when we were one, it was promised we would be one again. So, Yahweh promised, and his will be done."

Michael nodded.

"What are the six signs of Sibtala," he continued with his inquisition.

Zar indulged him. "The first sign was as Diaona had said, the alignment of the worlds. The second sign was the opening of the seal, causing the ground to open and granting you passage here.

"The third sign is the reunion of two soulmates separated by time, which I believe has already begun," Zar added. "Has it now sweet sister?"

Diaona replied. "It has."

Keith mimicked her response.

The two smiled at each other with knowing looks. Michael should not have been surprised by this, as he saw the attraction between the two of them, but soulmates? They didn't even know each other. It hasn't even been a month. It was a lot to take in. His head felt like it was spinning with everything he experienced this day.

"The fourth sign will be the awakening of The Wanders of Truth. They will walk again, reaching the corners of the earth to proclaim an end to the old world and the birth of a new one," Zar proclaimed.

"The birth of a new one," Michael whispered to himself.

"The fifth sign is the rebirth of an old religion. This will mark and reopen a lost temple for new followers. The fifth sign will also cause the unjustified deaths of a 1,000 humanidauns, which will anger Yahweh. This will bring about the sixth sign."

He leaned towards Keith and in a whispering tone, he spoke, "What is the sixth sign?"

Zar turned to look at Michael with a somber expression and sadness in his voice. Two humanidauns will give birth to a star child. This is the sign that will awaken all of us and brings us out of hiding and into the world once more," he explained.

Michael took note of the sadness in Zar's voice.

"That doesn't sound that bad, why are you sad," Michael asked.

Zar's somber mood confused Michael because he figured it would be a good thing if the other races were able to walk among them once more. Keith, however, was able to see past the words Zar spoke and understood their hidden meaning. He knew that everything needed an opposite to exist. To survive. To make sense in the world. If there is an "up," there must be a "down."

Diaona had been quiet, she too seemed to mirror Zar's expression.

194

Keith understood as well, leaving just Michael to figure it out.

"All of us, Michael. All of us," Zar said softly.

CHAPTER TWENTY-FOUR

Most people don't realize how our brains learn language. Obviously, sound is very important. Both animals and humans use the sounds we make to communicate.

It is through that communication that we share information, but it's more than that. Human speech and writing are very complex processes that takes years to learn.

Reena knew the words, but the spell didn't turn out the way she intended. Roland could see the increasing frustration on her face. He of course knew the answer, but to try and explain it to her would simply infuriate her.

Her brain was still hardwired to the old way of learning. Studying the books in front of her won't unlock the block she had in her mind. She had to bend, like a child bends.

She needed to be more flexible in her thinking. When we are children we have no choice but to be adaptable, as we grow older we seem to lose this ability. Roland might have lost it, too, had it not been for his rare form of autism.

Reena sat around the table, doing her best to read in the presence of a white, glowing sphere illuminating the entire room. It was somewhat distracting, but she was doing her best to deal with it. She had simply lost track of time while drowning herself in the pages of the current book. Reena looked exhausted and it was late. Roland walked over to Reena.

"You should try and get some sleep," Roland said concerned.

She shook her head. "You can get some sleep while I study."

She meant it, but Roland wasn't going to give in that easily. He moved closer and sighed softly before stopping a few feet from the table.

"We have time. There's no need to rush we-"

Reena cut him off. "No! Time is something I don't have!"

Roland stared at her for a moment then turned around and exited the room. Reena continued reading for a while, but the words on the page no longer made sense.

She tried to ignore the pang of guilt eating away at the walls of her stomach. The way she responded to Roland in such unruly manner was uncalled for.

Now that she thought about it, Roland never seemed to get emotional. It seemed strange, but for a brief moment she saw the pained look in his eyes before he left the room.

She had hoped she could handle it, but that wasn't going to be the case. She got up and walked towards the next room, where she was sure Roland had gone.

Roland had never known love before, although he had read books and watched movies on the subject.

He was now becoming familiar with the feeling, and it was overwhelming. The ancient Greeks described love as the madness of the gods, the phrase was lost on him until now. What a sad situation he found himself in. His thoughts and dreams were consumed by her.

He remembered every feature on her face, the smell of her on a primal level. It wasn't the perfume or soap she used but the smell of her sweat mixed with her clothes.

It was a scent he couldn't easily describe but he knew it as her. He didn't know how she felt about him, and part of him wasn't sure he wanted to know. If she didn't feel the same way, he wasn't sure he could bare the truth. Right now, she was with him.

They spent all their waking hours together, and he loved watching the expressions on her face when they learned something new together.

Roland was so consumed with his thoughts of Reena he didn't even realize he was casting a spell. A spell that came from his very soul, a ghostly image of Reena appeared before him wearing a beautiful white dress. She danced barefoot and laughed. How he loved her smile. Roland was so consumed with the dream he created that he didn't hear Reena come in the room.

"Roland are you in there," she asked.

She looked ahead and saw light emanating from a room, which was two rooms away from where she was standing. It prompted her to walk ahead quickly in hopes of seeing what was going on in there. She caught sight of Roland sitting on the floor and staring at an image of a woman floating slightly in the air. The image twirled around, revealing Reena's own face.

"Oh my God!" Reena screamed, prompting Roland to turn around to look at her.

The image of Reena slowly faded away. A myriad of emotions flash across Roland's face. So unaccustomed to feeling anything, he froze like a deer caught in headlights. He stared at her for a moment then tried to close and hide the marble notebook he had in his hands. The movement caught Reena's eyes and she quickly snatched the book from Roland and opened it. She began flipping through the notebook endlessly. It was dazzling and troubling at the same time.

On each page was a detailed drawing of Reena in different poses and with various expressions on her face.

"What is this?" Reena asked.

Roland refused to grace her with an answer and turned away.

She wasn't going to give up "Roland, I ask you, what is this?"

Reena walked over and looked Roland directly in his eyes. Roland's gaze was still peering at the floor. She held the book in front of him.

"For months I have been down here with you. Not once have you said anything to me. Why?"

Roland shook his head. "You will not understand."

"Try me," she demanded.

"It's a strange thing when you begin to care for someone. Do you know what I mean?" Roland finally asked, she nodded. Her answer came out as a whisper. "Yes."

Roland sighed and continued speaking. "It's even stranger when the last person in the world you would ever think of falling in love with, you do. Deep down you know she will never love you the way that you do because she's a different person."

Reena looked pale with shock. She had not seen that coming at all.

"So, it's easier to live in a fantasy than to face that reality. That way no one gets hurt. I'm sorry if I offended you," he apologized.

Reena was taken aback and overwhelmed. It was in that moment she realized that she truly cared for this man. Exactly when she had fallen in love with him she didn't know, but she had. She knew how hard it was for Roland to express himself to her and she wanted him to know that she felt the same way, too. Her eyes softened, and her mouth curled up to form a shy smile.

"You didn't offend me, Roland. Most men see me as a bitch. So that's what I give them. You see me in a way I hardly see myself. It's I that should apologize to you," Reena said compassionately.

She handed the notebook back to him and he took it from her without looking at her. He turned away slowly and began walking away until he heard her voice call out to him.

"Roland, where do you think you are going," she asked. "Don't you have a drawing to finish?"

Roland halted his steps and slowly turned around to see Reena unbuttoning her shirt. With a quick movement, the shirt fell to her shoulders, then the floor.

She unbuckled her pants and let them drop down to her ankles. She stepped out of her pants and towards Roland. He stood there just staring and admiring her, he was afraid to move. She walked over in just her bra and underwear and hugged him close.

Roland felt her pressing against his body in a manner that left him excited and uncomfortable all at the same time. Slowly, she wrapped her arms around his neck and eased her lips towards his until they locked in a kiss. She then kissed him on his left cheek.

Whispering into his ear, she said, "I am in the presence of the most brilliant linguist of our lifetime, but I don't understand why he has a hard time..."

She moved her head to the other side of Roland's face and kissed him on his right cheek.

" ...with the world's first language, love."

She leaned closer and kissed him on the lips once more.

"Love is the hardest language to learn," Roland confessed.

Reena chuckled loudly. "Thank God for that!"

She pinned him to a wall and slowly began unbuttoning his shirt. She kissed him passionately as he did the same to her without end. They both couldn't contain how they felt, and it was apparent as they journeyed ahead.

CHAPTER TWENTY-FIVE

It was late. Way past midnight, yet too early to be awake. Zachary's mind was restless, so he, too, was restless.

He could not sleep. He stood just outside of his tent looking at the night sky. It truly was a sight to behold. How can it be so dark that he could not see his hand in front of his face, and yet the night sky was alive.

He could see hundreds of stars, maybe thousands. He wished at that moment he was more of an astrophile, which is just a fancy word for someone who loves stargazing.

As a child, Zachary knew the names of a number of constellations, but he couldn't find them in the infinite sea of stars he stared at now. He pulled a cigar out of his pocket and smelled it.

Everyone thinks that Cuban cigars are the best, and they may very well be, but if you can't get your hands on them, what the hell is the point? Macanudo from the Dominican Republic was just heavenly.

Zachary knew that smoking these things would probably be the end of him, but we all have our vices, and he just couldn't resist the silky-smooth flavor of a good cigar. The scent calmed his nerves and allowed him to focus his mind. Zachary heard movement behind him. The smell of the cigar must have awoken Susan.

Donning a small white nightgown, Susan walked outside of the tent and make her way towards him in silence.

"It is late Zachary." Her words sliced through the darkness. "Why are you up?"

"You need not worry, dear. You can go back to sleep," Zachary replied, while trying not to act like he had been startled.

She could detect an edge of worry in his voice.

"What's wrong," she asked in a more serious tone.

"Everything is fine," he lied.

Years of being with the same person told her different.

She wasn't going to give in that easy. He definitely wasn't fine, and it worried her.

"Then why are you smoking? You only smoke when you feel like something's wrong."

He turned around to address her. "Have you any idea what a pain in the ass it is when someone knows you too well?"

She approached him, wrapping her arm around him and leaning her head on his shoulder.

"I think I'm losing control of this project," he confessed.

She let the statement hang in the air for a moment, knowing Zachary would eventually explain what he meant.

"Reena agreed to go down there to keep an eye on Dr. Misthos, and now she barely even comes up to the surface," he fumed. "Ralph is getting antsy, and I don't blame him, because the work is almost done, and the poor guy hasn't gotten laid in over six months."

"You are terrible," Susan chuckled.

"Not to mention that it's getting really bad out in the real world.

It's so peaceful here. No problems. There's nothing to worry about here."

Susan knew deep down that what he was talking about was just scratching the surface. There was something more eating away at him.

"What's really bothering you?" she inquired in a gentle, knowing tone.

"We're running out of money. Soon we'll have to let the whole world know about our discovery," he replied.

"So? This is what you've been waiting for. This discovery will make you famous. You'll be a king among men. You'll be able to do anything you want."

He extended his hand around her waist and shook his head. "I don't intend to be a king, but I want to know where the future might lead. Hopefully it will be somewhere good."

They both fell silent for a brief period before Susan spoke again.

"Zach. Please, for once, live for the moment. Forget about tomorrow and live for today! Can you do that? Do it for me," she advised. "More importantly, do it for yourself!"

"You are right," he whispered. "I'll give them until the end of the week, then we will all leave here with the promise of fortune and glory."

Zachary turned toward Susan, in a sweeping motion picking her up and carrying her to bed.

CHAPTER TWENTY-SIX

Gary could barely move, his whole body hurt. There was a pain in his heart that wasn't there before.

No matter how hard he tried to shake it, he knew deep down, something was terribly wrong. That's when the rage took over. He felt something inside him crack. It was as if someone dropped a bottle of beer on the floor to shatter in pieces.

The feelings he had ran cold out of him like beer from the broken bottle. He was empty inside. The uncontrollable need to exact punishment took over.

Deep down, he knew he wasn't going to live to see another day. However, there might be a chance for his family. He knew what he had to do.

The aero vessel had a streamlined hull designed to operate in a vortex of rotating destructive winds. The ship was equipped with an internal supply of air with four 10-terabyte drives. Although the vessel had a joystick to steer the ship, the computer did most of the flying. Perhaps flying is the wrong word, it is more of a controlled drop under savage conditions.

The vessel had no windows. Instead, cameras were mounted in strategic areas., Not so much to see, the cameras were used to interpret graphical data. The intel is then displayed on one of the six monitors in front of the pilot and co-pilot, showing 3D computer images of the terrain and numeric data values. It was one of Gary Marks greatest engineering achievements.

Gary bent his head towards the ground as he spat out some blood before speaking in low tone. "If I'm going to die here, so are these bastards!"

He sounded determined and looked it, too. He had thought it all through and it seemed like the only viable option. He could barely stand and was getting light-headed from his injuries and blood loss. He flipped a panel open and cut a blue wire before tucking it underneath a red one. As he closed the panel, exhaustion set in and he fell to the ground.

"Hey you! You better get the fuck up and finish," one of the guards watching him yelled.

"It's done," Gary stuttered. "The fucking thing is finished! Please let me see my wife and kid!"

The guard ignored him and took out his radio to speak into it.

"General, sir, the ship is finished."

The unmistakable voice of General Dubner replied. "Understood! Complete your assignment."

"Yes, sir," the guard responded before tucking away the radio and turning to look at Gary. "I guess you want to see your family now."

Gary watched the guard walk over to the monitor to turn it on. The black screen slowly faded to reveal a sharp image of Gary's wife and daughter slumped in their chairs. They were still, uncomfortably still. He looked at his wife's face and noticed that her eyes were fixed in an unblinking stare. His daughter's eyes were closed. Gary knew what it meant immediately.

He began to weep.

"You'll be happy to know that they didn't feel anything. It was painless. I'm sorry, sir, I wish things could have been different," the guard explained in a callous tone.

Gary kept his head low and did not look up. He heard the sound of the safety on the guard's gun click. Four loud bangs followed as the guard unloaded four bullets at point blank range into Gary. Two bullets entered his back and exited out of his chest, killing the man instantly. The other two shots were fired into Gary's head. It was overkill and unnecessary. Blood and brain matter were splattered all over the floor. It was clear, not only did this solider like killing, but he had also lost his soul some time ago.

———————

MILITARY BASE

GENERAL DUBNER'S OFFICE

No one knows what a soldier goes through unless they have been in the military themselves. There is a moral code that every soldier follows.

 In the end, all you have is the belief that what you are doing for your country is just and right.

It is a struggle when faced with the utter challenges of what the greater good may be, and how your decisions will affect future generations. It's absolutely vital we all have a shared interest in the outcome and that the future we imagine is one everyone can live with.

It's a future that should be better and brighter than our current existence. For the first time in 22 years as a soldier, General

Dubner doubted his mission and questioned the orders he was given.

A bottle of Royal Salute 32-Year-Old – Union of the Crowns sat open on his desk. It was a gift from the secretary of state for bravery in a top-secret confrontation on foreign soil. He never intended on opening it, then again, there were a lot of things he didn't intend on doing. Yet, here he was. Dubner filled his glass three-fingers neat and took a sip of the whiskey.

God damn was it good. It should be more than $400 a bottle. He was going to enjoy this while he could, but the mood turned sour when Mr. Levine entered his office.

"I see everything is going according to schedule," Mr. Levine hissed. "Tell your men to be ready by 0300. We'll attack at dawn. That way we'll have an audience."

The General simply took another sip from his glass and listened to the man. Levine looked at the General, his eyes trailing down to the glass of whiskey in his hand.

"What the hell are you doing drinking so early in the morning?"

"Fuck off Levine," General Dubner snapped. "My men are responsible for the deaths of 141 people! Americans! Families completely destroyed. You have no idea what it is to carry something like that around!"

Silence sat between them momentarily.

"Oh, but I do," Mr. Levine replied. "More lives have been destroyed by these hands. More than you can possibly imagine. Your way of thinking ended the minute our group assassinated

President Lincoln!"

General Dubner shook his head in disgust and dismay. He stared at Levine with contempt in his eyes. He looked at his drink. Taking hold of his glass, he drained the remainder of the whiskey in one gulp. "The country is as safe as it can be because we make it so," Mr. Levine continued. "The American dream is what we provide, so please spare me the dramatic behavior and just do what you're told!"

Mr. Levine rose out of his seat and headed for the door, looking at the General once before exiting, slamming the door behind him.

Left with his thoughts, General Dubner held three fingers to his glass and poured himself another drink. He held his drink up to the light, admiring the caramel color. Then he held the glass to his nose and inhaled the pear, woody aroma, finally sipped the thirty-year-old liquid letting it slowly burn down his throat. He smiled in appreciation before sighing and picking up his phone. He punched in a phone number and waited a moment before the call connected. "Yes, this is General Dubner. Your orders are to strike at dawn under code 111. Seven minutes into the attack, use the bomb and drop the device into the Fork. You have you orders. Good luck soldier. God be with you."

He hung up the phone and sighed. General Dubner got up from his desk and walked over to a mirror.

He was in his full Army Service Uniform, which is odd because around the base all of the soldiers are usually in their Army Combat Uniform.

He adjusted his uniform, making sure everything lined up

perfectly.

He then took a lint brush to his uniform, taking care everything looked pristine. Satisfied, he walked back to his desk and held up his glass in a toast.

"God be with you," he whispered to himself. He then drank the rest of the whiskey in one contented gulp. He placed the glass down on the desk and looked at himself in the mirror again. "I wish God was with me," he whispered.

General Dubner pulled out a compact SIG Sauer P320 pistol from the holster he wore at his side, placed the barrel of the gun to his temple and squeezed the trigger.

The bullet caused the General's head to jolt violently to the left. Blood splattered on the $400 bottle of Royal Salute 32-Year-Old – Union of the Crowns on his desk, his lifeless body fell to the ground.

CHAPTER TWENTY-SEVEN

Michael could not believe what was happening. He could not deny the things both he and Keith have seen but it was all happening too fast.

He needed time to sit and process what was going on. This group of angels, their excessive devotion to something out there, some greater all-knowing entity, didn't exist. At least that is what he believed.

It didn't make sense. They must be employing unethical and manipulative techniques, these were the tactics a cult would use. Yet, he also could not deny the feeling that kept plaguing him. The feeling of belonging to something greater than himself. The feeling of overwhelming peace did not compute in his scientific brain. His best friend is going to leave him.

Keith packed a small bag with belongings and knick-knacks he had brought with him from their camp near the village. It was all so surreal. His time in village and the people seemed so far away. His life on the surface before they entered the Fork felt like many years ago.

Keith watched Michael pace back and forth. Michael had been talking to him non-stop from the moment they had been left alone. He was confused and angry and rightfully so, it didn't make sense to him.

"Keith, I can't believe this is happening! You can't do this," Michael voiced in worrisome tone.

He stopped packing and looked at Michael. "It is okay Mike. Really,

I thought you would be happy for me."

Michael looked perplexed but carefully managed his thoughts before responding. "I am. Truly, I am, but everything is happening so fast. Let's pause and reflect on what we have just learned."

Keith resumed his packing before replying. He didn't know how to make Michael understand. He knew his friend just had his best interests at heart, but he simply was on another level of understanding that he could not easily explain with words. Michael stared at him, his eyes pleading with him to stay. The sentiment touched him.

"This is where I belong. At dawn, Diaona and I will be wed," Keith spoke without looking at Michael.

"You cannot be serious! This is a nightmare and I cannot believe this is happening! I feel like we are in The Twilight Zone," Michael fumed. "Did that crystal switch our personalities? Why am I the one in the dark and not you?"

Keith chuckled derisively and responded. "Life is funny, isn't it? Just when you get into a routine...Bam! Things change."

"No shit," Michael said sardonically.

Michael was scared and frustrated. He didn't know what to do. He was moments away from losing his colleague, confidant and best friend. He would be left alone in this place.

Now he knows how the Marshall family felt in that old television series Land of the Lost. He loved watching old re-runs of that show as a little kid, then as an adult the whole idea of the show was silly and kind of ridiculous. The truth was indeed stranger than fiction.

Sensing Michael's thoughts, Keith broke the nervous silence.

"Michael, listen to me. It's what you have been trying to teach me almost all of my life. You have always been the big brother I never had," Keith explained. "Now, in this moment, I understand. I am afraid to breathe because I may lose this feeling. We have been studying and learning together, unlocking the doors to mysteries just to find another door. By unlocking that door, we opened another realm of possibilities, which are endless. Truly endless! Anything is possible, Michael! Anything! I know I sound like a madman, but some of your questions will be answered by dawn's first light. I promise."

Michael knew what was coming next and he didn't want to say goodbye. He walked over to the window to look at the gorgeous garden before him. A bright blue sky with the golden rays of the sunshine scattered around the clouds. Keith walked closer and took a few seconds to share the view with Michael.

"I know you feel like things are ending, and to be honest, some things are. It's also the start of something new. Now please, I'm nervous as hell and I want to look good for my future wife. Will you help me?"

The angst and worry that plagued Michael slowly drained away from his body, replaced with a feeling of hope and resolve. The logical side of his brain told him it was impossible to stop the waves of change.

He just had to go with the flow.

Michael wiped the worry off his face and nodded. "I will be honored, my friend. Although I have to admit, I'm the one scared."

"Me and you both brother...me and you both," Keith replied.

The two laughed as Keith walked over to a chest and pulled out a white robe, holding it up for Michael to see.

"This is what I have to wear to the wedding! Any idea which side is the front?" The two laughed as Keith got dressed.

CHAPTER TWENTY-EIGHT

If they pulled this off, everything about what we believe in and what is possible will change forever.

Roland knew that everything he has done was leading to this point. Now that they were actually going to try it frightened and excited him all at the same time.

The people in those crystal coffins were still for all these centuries, perfectly preserved. Could they really be alive and just in stasis? The things these people know and would be able to share with the world would be unbelievable.

With all the advances in science, no one has ever attempted anything like this. It might be possible to live forever.

The thought was daunting. Somehow the practice of magic was forgotten, or was it? The things he could do now practically made him a god.

There were things he figured out that he wouldn't even share with Reena. Should he even share this knowledge with everyone?

We already possess the power to destroy the world. The Bulletin of the Atomic Scientists advanced the symbolic Doomsday Clock to one minute to midnight, bringing us that much closer to the apocalypse when a number terror groups became organized.

If any one of those groups get their hands on a nuke, it would be the end for all of us. What will happen if I reintroduced magic into the world, Roland thought to himself. He believed for the most part that people were good and decent. He had to believe that with all power comes responsibility. He knew what he had to do.

"How are you coming along my dear," he asked Reena, who was reading across the table from him in an ornate red robe. His powers seemed limitless. Roland had created the robes they wore using the magic. He looked at the bodies encased in their crystal coffins and had duplicated the outfits. He somehow manipulated the fibers and cloth seemingly out of thin air but of course it was more than that, he had created the outfits out of pure energy. A task that if he really thought about, should have scared him to death. Luckily, he was so enamored by the woman sitting in front of him, that he didn't give it much contemplation.

He admired the outfit along with a gold headband that secured her locks. The headband had a ruby affixed in its center. He looked at his green robe and smiled at her when she met his gaze.

"I really don't know," she confessed.

"I'm so excited I can hardly stand still," Roland gushed.

They were both scared, it was apparent on their faces and by their demeanor. They had both spoken at length on what could happen if they pulled it off.

"They've been around since the Renaissance or even maybe longer than that," Reena sounded enthusiastic.

"Even if I die now, I'll die happy," Roland revealed.

Reena folded her arms and frowned. "Don't say such things! Our lives are about to begin anew."

"If we were to follow the rules of the Torah, we are already married," she explained.

Roland smiled thinking about the intimate nights they shared together learning.

"How is it you know some much about the Hebrew religion," he inquired.

"Before my son's illness, I was a true believer and a practicing Jew," she said.

He walked closer to her and hugged her tightly from behind. She planted a kiss on his neck and cheek softly in return.

"And what about now?" Roland questions. "After all you've seen. The scrolls? The walls? The power?"

"I don't know what to believe. I do know that I am happy. I know this might sound silly or it might not be the right time to bring it up but," she paused.

"What is it? You can tell me," Roland encouraged her.

A tear rolled down her cheek before she spoke. "My son was very dear to me and now he's gone. This power, will it cure me? Could it have saved my son?"

Roland nodded.

"Well, we can't stay down here forever. As much as I would like to, I need to know what your plans are for the future," she said nervously.

Roland had been expecting and hoping for this question. He knew how he felt, but it was hard for him to put into words. He spent his free time practicing this response in the hopes that she shared his feelings. It was difficult for him, but he turned her around until she was looking directly into his eyes.

"For the future, I plan to help you find a cure. I plan to take you as my new wife. If you will have me as your husband, I will find a home for the two of us to live. For the first time in my life, I am truly happy."

Reena's heart raced, and she felt a joy she had not felt in a very long time. For the first time in a long time, she felt hopeful.

"Never in my life have I been more in love than I am right now," she admitted.

The two shared a passionate kiss. Reena then looked at Roland's robe and used her hand to smooth out a wrinkle near his chest. She looked up at him.

"Do you think it's too early to be dressed like this," Reena asked.

Roland looked at his robe and chuckled. "It is too late to worry about that now, don't you think? We need to cast the spell exactly one hour after dawn."

"Well, it's late afternoon now. Chances are we won't have to worry about the others coming down. In the morning, however, Ralph always comes down the first chance he gets," Reena reminded him.

Roland didn't look worried.

"Are you ready to take our lives to the next level?"

A sudden voice from the room startled them both, causing them to jump. Reena laughed out in nervous fear. Roland kept silent, trying to figure out where the sound was coming from. It was a hollow, scratching sound like a ghost. He scanned the room and then spotted the C.B radio on the floor.

The voice came once again in an animated tone. "Roland! Reena! Come in! Are you there?"

Roland took his time to pick up the receiver. "Yes Zachary, we are here."

"Great! I have a wonderful news for the both of you," he chimed from the other end.

Reena walked to the other side of the room and stood by Roland.

"Pack your bags both of you, tonight will be the last time you'll ever spend in that dungeon!"

"What? But we haven't finished transcribing the walls yet," he protested in shock.

They waited for a response, but Zachary took his time. The air suddenly felt stifling for the two of them.

"That's okay! You can finish up in a month or two from now, but I have a big news conference set up in Geneva next week," he sounded certain. "By the time we break the news to the world, when we break this news to the world, we'll be able to get millions in funding! It's only right the two of you be there to share in the glory!"

They couldn't leave, not yet. Roland's mind scrambled for a solution to this new dilemma.

"I would really appreciate if we could spend just one more day down here! I'm really close to breaking open something big down here," Roland pleaded.

"I'm afraid that's impossible. Ralph has already left with one of the jeeps and most of the artifacts! He's returning tomorrow with a helicopter to pick us up," Zachary declined. "Besides, Reena must be tired and ready to get out of there."

Reena relieved Roland of the radio and said the first thing that came to her mind. "Zach! I'm fine! But you should really reconsider letting us stay just one more day! Please! We're on to something that will blow your mind away!"

"What is this thing you've discovered," Zach sounded curious.

Reena knew Zachary better than Roland did and knew how to push the man's buttons. She knew what made him tick almost as well as Susan. She looked at Roland for confirmation before getting a nod from him, urging her to go on.

"We found a fourth scroll that speaks of a treasure room, but we don't know the location yet," she explained.

"This is fantastic! Well, I can't give you another day, but we'll keep this a secret until we can dig for it! Both of you have done an excellent job! I'll be down to get you tomorrow! See you then! Over and out."

Roland looked at her and sighed.

"Why did you say that?" he asked.

"I thought I could get another day out of him if he thought there was some money down here," she explained.

He understood her reasoning. With a look and knowing smile, he assured her everything would be fine.

"What if he comes down in the middle of the spell?" she asked.

"Not to worry my love, this is meant to be and there is nothing he can do to stop us."

Reena felt content and returned to the table to continue studying her spell in preparation.

CHAPTER TWENTY-NINE

What makes a government corrupt? It's a question that seems easy to answer, but there are so many degrees of corruption that sometimes it's hard to see. It all comes down to just two things. Money and power.

It is something we have known for a long time, and yet no one is completely innocent. It's so hard to be a super power. The United States is perhaps one of the greatest countries in the world, but as great as we are, we also suffer from corruption.

Mr. Levine knew this. He knew that we sometimes had to look the other way in order for things to happen. There is a price to pay for money and power.

Something most Americans never realize. They get up, go to work, eat, fuck, then go to sleep and repeat the process day in and day out.

They say ignorance is bliss. It's true. I do what I do so the American dream stays alive. In case you're wondering, Denmark is the least corrupt nation in the world, but what has Denmark done? Exactly my point, nothing of note. Afghanistan, Iraq and Somalia are at the very bottom.

If the rumors are to be believed, the Fork represents a new area to explore for resources and revenue.

Plans were being put in place around the camp as men raced around putting things in place as they readied the planes and tanks for war. The personnel donned black fatigues, and a soldier raced to meet a metallic vehicle to check the cables harnessed around it. A man stood next to the ship, waiting for the soldier who walked over briskly.

"Everything is secure, sir," the solider reported.

Levine looked at him and nodded. "Good! Attach this baby to the B-52."

He read the label on the soldier's left breast pocket, and the name was "Springer." The man walked away before Mr. Levine turned east to wave at a man in a flight uniform. The man he recognized by the name Major James Malkin walked over briskly.

"Rally your men, Major," Mr. Levine paused momentarily. "Or should I say General? I hear you are up for a promotion."

They both shared a smile and the Major blew a whistle, which got the attention of a man standing in a tower far ahead. He pulled an air raid horn that blared throughout the bunker, causing the men to stop what they were doing and line up in perfect rows. The Major waited for them all to settle before he addressed them.

"Good morning! Normally the General would be making this speech, but he's been called away by the president in order to serve his country. That is why you men are here, to serve your country for the greater good. This is not a war against another country, it's a situation that needs to be rectified. It's a matter of this great nation's security. We protect America and help it remain great! So, if you men have any doubts, leave here now with a clear conscience. Don't, however, betray this man's army, your president and the people you have been chosen to protect by not being able to fulfill your obligations here today! Are you up for the challenge?"

The men yelled "yes, sir" in acknowledgment.

The Major continued.

"What we are doing may seem immoral. I'm not going to lie to you, some of the shit you will be doing is immoral as hell! It is, however, for the greater good of the country! Your mission is to fly into the area known as Devil's Fork. Under the guise of fake fire fight, it will appear that America is fighting against the terrorist group known as the "Black Dagger." We will defeat them and save the day. Do any of you have questions? Good! Remember, you'll be firing blanks at the group posing as the Black Dagger, so make it look real. A second team will come in afterwards and plant the cadavers. You have your orders! We move out in 10 minutes!"

The soldiers scattered in every direction like ants in bid to finish up the tasks at hand. Mr. Levine, who had been a spectator for the major's speech, seemed to materialize out of the darkness. That was one of Mr. Levine's many talents. He walked over to the Major from behind.

"That was quite a speech. I wasn't aware you were using blanks," he said with a baffled tone. "Do you think it will look real?"

"Who said anything about blanks?" Major James Malkin chuckled.

Mr. Levine grinned. "I like your style, Major."

CHAPTER THIRTY

The garden was full of people. Although very different from himself, Michael decided they were still just people. People with wings who have just happened to live for centuries, albeit. The thought made him smile. They were all gathered together to recognize the amalgamation of two people as partners, a special union, a marriage. This ritual between two people had kind of lost it's true meaning in the world where Michael is from. People divorce as much as they marry. Sex, for the most part, had become just a physical, chemically charged high people engaged in.

Here below, however, was a true matrimony. You could feel it in the air and see it in the faces of the people here. It wasn't just two people deciding to live together and throw caution to the wind. This was a true union of body, mind and soul. He was suddenly envious of his friend and wondered if he would ever find happiness like that. He thought about religion. For years, he dismissed the ten commandments in the bible. A set of rules to keep mankind in check. Reflecting on them now, he realized how perfect and unique the laws were. Especially the sin of adultery, a sin so bad its listed twice. We have become lost in our pursuit of happiness. Hopefully, it's not too late.

It is early dawn, and although it's still dark in the garden, it's also alive with people walking and talking in low whispers. There is a static charge in the air and there is this overwhelming feeling that something great is about to happen. Michael's thoughts were broken by the sound of an angelic voice in his ear. He turned to face a stunningly beautiful woman with wavy raven hair. He barely noticed her wings flex behind her as he gazed into her emerald-

225

colored eyes. For the moment, he almost forgot how to speak.

"Hello, I am known as Mitra," she introduced herself.

Michael nodded respectfully. "Hi, my name is Michael."

She smiled and looked towards Keith. "You must be proud of your friend this day."

Michael smiled at her, silently entertained the thought that Keith might be on to something.

"Indeed I am. Where I come from, we call this a wedding," Michael said.

"Here, we call it a joining. It marks much more than the joining because today we will await the sign."

"The birth of the Star Child," Michael said matter-of-factly.

"Yes. It will mark the new beginning. We can then live among you as we once did," Mitra said with excitement.

Michael didn't share Mitra's enthusiasm. In fact, he harbored this feeling of dread growing deep inside him. The people here were so trusting, almost innocent in their thinking. The world they knew has long been forgotten. They might not like what they find. The people above, the people he knew, were ugly, self-absorbed, technology-driven creatures who barely believed in themselves, let alone an all-powerful being. Those that believed in a god believed that their god and their god alone was the only one that existed. Damn the rest of them to hell. His people have fought wars for thousands of years based on what they believe. The whole world had become that island in the book the Lord of the Flies. The people are like those frightened children, fighting to stay and terrified

226

of the darkness that lives inside of them.

Michael spoke solemnly. "Yes, that sounds nice, but the world we live in might not be ready. I fear for your people as well as mine."

"You look at things only on the surface," Mitra spoke with sadness now.

"How should I think?" Michael questioned.

Mitra tilted her head and gazed at Michael with a quizzical look on her almost-flawless face.

"What an odd question," Mitra mused. "With your heart and soul of course." Mitra gestured to everything around them as she spoke. "To use all six senses at once. To be connected to every living being on the planet above and below."

"I wish I could think like that."

Mitra turned to Michael and gently stroked his face. A woman he didn't know was truly concerned for his wellbeing.

"What is stopping you?" she asked with a whimsical look.

Michael searched through himself for an answer and thought about what he alone experienced in the Star Chamber. He was touch by something. He did not want to admit what he experienced. He still didn't tell Keith what had transpired because he could not explain it. The entity felt good. The being, if it was truly God, meant him no harm. For now, that was enough. He struggled to believe and felt he was unworthy. The guilt flooded through him. Angelic voices came to his ears, as if to tell him all would be well. He cast his thoughts aside as people in the group began singing.

"It is about to begin," Mitra whispered.

He watched as Mitra took his hand. She joined the others in a chorus, singing in the language that sounded so beautiful that brought tears to Michael's eyes. Then it happened. The sun began to rise. It something Michael had witnessed only a couple of times in his life and just then he wondered why? There is nothing like watching the sunrise, it is a completely different event when you can see the sun rise out of the water. The sun suddenly began to appear over the edge of the water. There was almost a hum or a rumble in the air that accompanied this event. The sound must have been imagined, or if it did occur, it happened in the mind. The temperature rose at least 10 degrees and the garden came alive. The garden's colors brought forth its beauty.

Keith and Diaona walked into the garden hand in hand, both wearing white silk. They continued their walk until they were in the center of the garden. Before them, in the center of the group, stood Zar ready to officiate the ceremony.

"Today is the beginning! A new day has come," Zar cried out.

Those around cheered wildly.

He continued. "On this day, it is my honor to present to you the two who are to be joined. Linked by Yahweh for all time to help make the world a better place."

Michael looked at his friend and noticed the smile on his face. He was the only one who truly knew Keith, but he could see and feel the love and admiration these people felt for his friend.

"Keith who is not one of us, we accept with open arms. Let me be the first one to call him brother," Zar smiled.

Zar moved closer to Keith and gently planted kisses on the man's cheeks. Keith felt a tear trickle down his face as he looked over to Michael. Michael held some tears in his eyes, too, but managed to keep himself in check. It was at that moment something opened in Michael, something deep inside of his soul.

"This is beautiful," Michael said in their native tongue without realizing it. "I am so proud to be here right now."

Mitra agreed. "Yes, it is indeed beautiful to see beings of different races opening their hearts towards one another."

Michael wasn't aware at first that Mitra had not replied to him in English but in her language. Like water slowly seeping through a crack in a wall, Michael came to the realization that he understood. His mind comprehended, his soul, his essence was finally awake. He looked at Mitra with shock and bewilderment, he was going to ask her how this was possible. Before he could form the question into words, Mitra grabbed his hand in understanding and answered.

"With the heart open to one another, all things are possible," she said.

They share a long smile before turning back to listen to Zar speak. Michael felt as high as kite and wasn't even sure he could contain his joy.

"We pray and give thanks to Yahweh for this moment, as it will remain in our hearts and memories forever." Zar laughed and turned to Keith and Diaona. "Have you both prepared your vows?"

They replied "yes" in unison. Zar granted them the stage to speak. Diaona appeared nervous as she looked at Keith and smiled. She knelt before him and he knelt before her. She held his right hand to her lips before kissing it gently.

She began her vows slowly.

"Sweet man that I will call Datela, my soulmate, my other half that has walked in darkness and now has stepped into the light. Time for us has no meaning for I just met you, yet I have known you all of my life. Forever joined will I be to you in life and death my love, and it will never weaken. I am yours."

Keith had never felt that emotional before, as tears began rolling down his eyes. She had spoken the words in perfection and melted his heart in the process. It was his turn and he didn't even know what he had to say could even compare to her eloquent words.

He cleared his throat to begin.

"Out from the darkness and into the light. My soul cries for the first time. I am a man who has found love. I face you now with my mind and heart open to you. I trust you fully and give myself completely to you, who I will call Datela, my soulmate. All I ask from you is that you love me the way I love you, for time is precious to me. I fear the future, but I will walk to the ends of   the earth with you and no one else. I love you."

Their vows were wonderful, and the crowd cheered wildly upon receiving them. Those around began singing.

CHAPTER THIRTY-ONE

The news no longer provided just information, now the news could be used as a platform to manufacture opinion. The people became oversaturated with it, numb to the horrors of war, murder and catastrophe. Something that happens half way around the world can be known to the rest of the world in seconds. To hold the public's attention, the news needed to shock and entertain. Carl Foster, a reporter with WWN, The World-Wide News Network, knows this all too well. He must have done something to someone to piss them off, because he was stuck covering The Devil's Fork. The bird's-eye view of the Fork was mesmerizing though. It resembled that of a forked tongue. It ran for miles, projecting its beauty in a more efficient manner than the Grand Canyon. On the northern side of the Fork were no fewer than 20 news vans with skeleton crews waiting for something, anything, to happen.

The Fork was a non-story, old news. Carl was a bit of an asshole, and that didn't help him with his current situation. So, it's no surprise that he is taking out his frustration on his assistant. Carl stood a couple of feet away from the fork and stared into its depths. He took a sip of coffee then immediately spit it out on the ground.

"Shit! Damn it, Pierre, how many times do I have to tell you something before it sinks in that thick head of yours?" Carl fumed. "If you are going to be my assistant, you have to know I require a decent cup of coffee in the morning. You work with the big boys now! WWN is the biggest news network in the world. Here are two words for you to remember, "flavored coffee." Go ahead, say it with me."

Carl chastised his assistant so loudly other people in the area stopped to take notice.

Pierre tried to apologize but wasn't given the opportunity, as Carl's mocking was relentless.

"Say it with me Pierre, say it with me." Carl gesticulated and urged the young man to speak the words "flavored coffee" with him.

They muttered the absurd phrase together three different times before he sent him on his way to right the snafu.

"And let's get the coffee before the seven o'clock news! How hard could it be! We're practically in Mexico and just hop, skip and a jump away from Columbia for Christ sake," Carl yelled after him. Pierre walked away fuming with anger and made a mental note to spit in Carl's coffee. Dennis Morris, a reporter from a rival news network, observed the whole incident and yelled at Carl.

"Hey! Foster! Give the kid a break," Dennis protested. "He is out here to learn how to be a journalist! Not your fucking piss boy!"

"Don't tell me you're jealous Morris," Carl bellowed. "I'm not the reason you're always one step behind me."

Dennis didn't respond to Carl, instead he instructed his camera-man to set up his equipment.

Carl ridiculed the man as he approached him. "It's great when you think about it! That's why I'm here and you there!"

He gestured with his hand, indicating that he was at a higher level in his career than Dennis.

"Look Morris! There you are, right under the loser' line. Hey, let me give you some advice. You should really just pack up your shit and go home," he continued.

Dennis had just about tuned out the man's voice when a young boy ran up to him and shoved a piece of paper into his hand. The boy then took off running in the opposite direction.

He looked at the boy wryly and slowly opened the note. In bold black script the words "The Black Dagger also uses a Fork" was scribbled on the paper. Dennis looked up just in time to see the boy run past Carl, who was still ranting.

"Hell! The truth is that, some people have it, and some don't. I've got it! I'm on fire," Carl boasted.

No sooner had Carl finished his sentence when his body suddenly exploded, sending his parts flying indistinguishably everywhere. What was left was literally on fire. Dennis slowly turned around to see the cameraman pointing his camera at the spot were Rubin had been standing. The little red light at the front of the camera winked at him. Dennis could not believe his eyes. Chaos erupted all around them.

"Did you get that?" he asked his cameraman in shock. "Oh my God, please tell me you were recording!"

The cameraman nodded. "You bet your ass I did!"

Dennis felt guilty and happy all at the same time. Smiling from ear to ear, he ran to a spot that seemed safe, his cameraman followed. Heavy machine gun fire and explosions bellowed out all around them.

"Go live now," Dennis screeched. "On me in 3...2....1..."

He waited a few seconds as the chaos continued around them. He watched and waited. His cameraman gave him the thumbs up and he straightened his tie to proceed.

"I'm Dennis Morris! You're watching WTAZ News on the go!

All hell has just broken out! I just received this note from a small child that The Black Dagger terrorists are responsible for this latest attack! The target, Devil's Fork!"

The cameraman pans to get a shot of the chaos and mayhem going on behind Dennis.

"Get three to five minutes of footage then we will go for the van," Dennis yelled out.

The cameraman nodded and recorded the carnage erupting all around them. A mortar shell landed a little too close for comfort; they managed to stay clear of the blast radius and crawled towards the news van. The two men jumped into the van and drove away from the battle to a safer spot.

"Cut together a montage clip of the battle, I want to go live again in 10," Dennis ordered. The cell phone rang, causing both men to nearly jump out of their boots. Dennis picked it up and spoke immediately.

"Yeah! What's the word," he asked?

He recognized the caller to be Barry, his boss.

Barry responded immediately. "You got the jump on everybody kid, our ratings just went through the roof! You stay there and record everything! You hear me! And watch out for those bastards over at the WWN! They will try to take the glory from you!"

Dennis looked out the window where Rubin had been standing. He lit a cigarette, took a puff, and smiled. "I wouldn't worry about that."

Something exploded near them. It rocked the van, sending dust and debris everywhere. High above them, unseen and beyond the clouds, a large B-52 bomber was flying over the Devil's Fork. The pilot contacted Command Central.

"This is eagle to Command Central, preparing to drop the egg in one minus two minutes and counting. Over," the pilot cried into his mouthpiece.

"You are cleared to drop the egg in the nest." The response came from the Command Central.

CHAPTER THIRTY-TWO

Everything is connected, to everything else. That's what Roland kept telling himself. He was never a religious person as a child, but he now knew without a doubt that God is real. He had read that magic and those that practiced it were evil, perhaps what he was doing now shouldn't be called magic, but he didn't have another word for it. Good and bad, up and down, yin and yang it's all there in front of him, it's all real. The rewards, as well as the consequences. With every level there is another devil. Roland realized the choice was his. He could choose to be good or bad. That was a choice everyone has. This is the great sin he realized. The moment right before Adam bit into the apple. If he did this, it would change everything. He read the stories, he knew what was written in the text. This moment might very well end the stalemate. It was time. Time for the entire world to finally wake up. He made his decision. He hoped, he prayed, it was the right one.

Roland and Reena made the preparations needed in the Tomb Chamber in the Temple of Goulaumx. They lit four torches and placed them in the four corners of the room. They poured circles of salt around each of the three coffins. Roland looked at the salt. As a child, his mother was obsessed with stones and minerals and their properties. Salt was supposed to have protection, healing and purification powers. Months ago, he would have laughed at the thought, but he had seen and been exposed to things beyond the imagination. He remembered the history of salt and its importance. Salt was so valuable that the Romans used to pay their soldiers with it. Most people don't even realize that the word "salary" has its root in the Latin word for salt. It amazed Roland that people no longer cared about the past and the secrets it held. The heat of the room brought Roland back to his senses.

Roland wiped off the beads of sweat that were rolling down his forehead.

He turned to look at Reena. "It is time…are you prepared?"

She hesitated but finally responded. "I think so."

Roland took a deep breath before speaking again.

"This is the most complicated spell I have ever attempted. I don't know what will happen if I mess up. If something happens to me, know my heart. Know that I love you and that no matter what happens the last couple of months have been the best of my life."

She placed her finger to his lip and held his hand. "Roland, I am scared, this is like something out of a dream."

He held her hand tightly and assured her that all will be well. He could see the love she had for him in her eyes and he showed her how much she meant to him, too.

"I love you." He said with a smile as he stroked her face. "It's okay. Don't worry, and no matter what happens, continue reading the incantation. Let's begin."

Reena smiled back. "I love you, too."

"Remember what to do if Zachary should interrupt us," he asked her.

She smiled and nodded. He turned and began tracing symbols in the air.

"Teas be ji frok! Leza ja lo mar! O sa deya rojar," Roland muttered.

Reena mirrored the symbols he was drawing and responded with her own chants. "Peaba To alou! Jena ka seede! Fia Cola Meda!"

Roland continued drawing the symbols faster, muttering the chants endlessly.

"He if so pela! Gar eve au woluam! Osdi ieru fegu! Daoru bedyeh. Aioew qued bengali!"

The coffins in the room began glowing as they radiated blue light. The flames on the torches went wild, too, and burned brightly as a current of wind began sweeping around the room. They were so engrossed in the ceremony that they didn't notice that they were no longer alone in the chamber. A voice called out to them, echoing from the other room.

"I hope the two of you are decent," Zachary called out.

He walked towards the chamber, seeing an eerie bright blue light glowing from within. Fearing the worst, Zachary ran towards the chamber. As he got closer, he heard the chanting and raced towards the door.

"What the hell is going on," he demanded.

Reena turned to look towards the door. She muttered a word and traced the equivalent symbol in the air.

"Dalreme," she yelled. With her words, a wall of fire grew around Zachary, restricting his movement.

They were all in danger, Zachary thought to himself. Months of digging and excavation and now they were all going to die in a fire.

He could not believe his eyes. Zachary backed up in confusion then screamed out in absolute terror.

"Reena! Roland! Help me! What in God's name is happening!"

They ignored him. Roland drew the incantation to a close by speaking the final words, "Satar woja De aloe baysid! Geridoman! Ukrostan! Albata!"

Michael was happy for his friend Keith and the decision he made. What he did, what he feels must be amazing for him. Michael was dancing with Mitra, but his thoughts consumed him. This indeed was an amazing journey, one the world will talk about for years to come. Part of him just wanted to go home. He needed some normality back in his life. Yet how would he get back, the ship was damaged beyond repair as far as he knew. There was no way back. Keith was going to make a home of this place, this paradise. What am I going to find back home? Perhaps this is fate just telling me what I already know. There is nothing really for me back there. There is so much I can learn, as well as teach. Mitra's touch brought him back to reality.

"I decided that I'm going to stay. I like it here," he said to her.

Mitra looked at him with a smile. "That's too bad I was thinking of leaving. To feel the real wind blow through my hair as I fly through the sky."

"What do you mean?" he inquired.

"Don't you know," she asked.

"No."

"All of this around you. All that you see here is done through magic. What you see is from the world above. It is our memories enhanced by the magic."

Michael stared at her in amazement. He had always guessed it was something, he thought eventually he would be able to explain it with science. Magic. It was hard to accept but somehow made sense.

"This doesn't exist in the world above. I hate to say this, but we have distorted the world you remember. It's not even remotely the same."

She smiled at him tenderly. "All things change. It is the way. We will either change our situation or change ourselves."

Michael grinned and thought of what she said earlier. "Magic? It's all so amazing!"

The area around the Fork had turned into a bloodbath, and the news networks had cameras on the action, soaking up every last drop of destruction and broadcasting it live to the world. However, for the solider who had boots on the ground, confusion and horror spread over the battlefield. Several of them started to realize that something was terribly wrong.

Dennis found shelter within the comfort of the WTAZ news van.

"It is a bloodbath here at Devil's Fork. Reports have come in stating that a joint effort between the United States and United Nations Military are trying to end the violence quickly. Details are few. As an eyewitness to these events as they occur, I can only state for sure that the body count is high on both sides."

A man dressed in the same garb as the Black Dagger typically wears looked perplexed as he ran towards two soldiers from the United Nations Military. "These are real bullets in the gun for Christ's sakes. I am an American!"

The two United Nations Military soldiers took aim, but before they could fire, a bullet pierced the shoulder of the man dressed in black, sending him to the ground. He summoned the strength to get back up to begin running again when more bullets tore through his chest and back.

"I have a wife...you're making a mistake," he cried out in his last words as blood trickled out of his mouth.

His eyes rolled back, and his last breath escaped his lips.

One of the United Nations Military soldiers looked to the other.

"Was he speaking in English," he asked.

The other soldier shrugged his shoulders. "I think he said he had a wife." The two men took aim and opened fire at the other men dressed in black running all over the place.

High above, and sheltered by the clouds, the bomber dropped its cargo into the Fork, followed by a missile. The ship and missile flew at the same pace but spread far apart from one another. As the missile struck the ground and exploded, the fireball and debris that followed permitted the ship to fly into the Fork undetected. The pilot, Major Malkin spoke in to the radio.

"This is Major James Malkin and we have made it into the Fork," the pilot relayed his message to the Command Central.

The ship traversed easily through the Fork, almost like a guided missile. The first ten thousand feet was easy. As the ship fell, it shook against the wind.

"We are getting close to the wall. Move ten degrees to your left," Lieutenant Todd Parker instructed.

Major Malkin obeyed by hitting the afterburners to maneuver the ship away from the wall. The ship headed towards the center and down towards the other wall in the process.

"You're over! Shut down," the Lieutenant warned.

Major Malkin did his best, but the controls failed. "It isn't responding damn it!"

He continued to hit the button tirelessly but got no response.

"Use the other burner," Lieutenant Parker advised.

"It is not fucking working damn it! I—"

The ship crashed into the wall and exploded before he could finish.

———————

It was truly a celebration unlike anything Michael and Keith had ever experienced before in their life. The group gathered in the garden, indulging themselves in the pleasures of life. Drinking a punch wine, singing song and expressing the many different levels of love.

Michael fed Mitra grapes. She looked up into Michael's eyes, her head on his shoulder as her wings embraced the two of them like a blanket.

"You do this well," Mitra said as she smiled at him.

"Thank You. I am your humble servant," Michael joked.

They were enjoying each other's company when someone yelled and pointed towards the sky. Everyone looked up to the orange and blue light, which flared brightly then died out.

"It is the sign! Yahweh has spoken," Mitra exclaimed.

Everyone around fell to their knees immediately and began praying. They raised their hands to the sky.

Keith looked to his wife and spoke. "It has begun!"

The flames swept around Zachary, keeping him at bay. It didn't make any sense. A strong current of air whipped around the chamber. It kept Zachary cool, but where the hell was it coming from! Zachary fell to his knees. He wept openly and screamed at the top of his lungs. Was he going insane? He watched Reena and Roland chant in some strange language and dressed in strange robes. Where did they get robes! Zachary frantically thought to himself.

Reena finished her incantation.

"Yea I beto gresa! Poaje Saui fiash! Abroutesell!!"

The last word she screamed activated the spell.

The crystal coffins exploded, sending shards of crystals flying up in the air. The broken pieces floated above their heads, as if they were in zero gravity. Then, the crystal shards started sticking together like magnets. They fused together creating a giant star shaped crystal. Speechless, Zachary just gazed at the newly

243

formed crystal floating above them. The stone began to glow a pale white light, which got brighter with each passing moment. Movement caught his eye and Zachary gasped. The three occupants of the coffins stood there alive and well. The wind blowing around the room doused the light from the torches, then the strange, magical wind disappeared completely. The only light in the room is now coming from the crystal. The woman looked at her companions.

"It has been a long time." The woman said.

The woman turned and looked at Reena and smiled. "So, this is the beginning."

GREENFIELD MEMORIAL HOSPITAL

DELIVERY ROOM

5:00 A.M

The delivery room is packed with doctors and nurses. They are helping a woman named Pamela Grieco who is in the middle of giving birth.

"Okay, Pam, you're so close and I can see the child's head, but you need to give me a hard push," Dr. Hirsch urged.

Pamela screamed and moaned as she tried to push. The lights in the room dim a bit. Her husband, Ted, is by her side, holding her hand and coaching her on.

"You are doing great Pam...I'm so proud of you," Ted whispered softly to his wife.

She pushed some more, while feeling the child ease out from within her thighs. The lights above flicker and dim again. One of the nurses looked up at the light for a second before returning her attention back to the patient.

"You're almost there," Dr. Hirsch cheered.

Pamela gave one big push and screamed. The baby was born. Dr. Hirsch looked at Ted and smiled.

"Would you like to do the honors of cutting the cord," he asked.

Ted nodded no in response. Dr. Hirsch cut the cord and then expertly tied it off. He cleaned the baby with a towel, then handed the child to the nurse.

"Mr. and Mrs. Grieco, you are the proud parents of a healthy baby boy," the doctor smiled at them.

———————

THE SCOTTISH HIGHLANDS

MORNING

A little girl pointed into the distance and towards the loch. The sight of a creature can be seen emerging from within the depths of the waters for a brief moment, before it disappeared again beneath the mass of water and out of sight.

———————

YELLOWSTONE PARK

In a remote part of the woods, a pair of humanoid arms break through the surface of the earth. A creature that is part man and part beast, with hindquarters legs and the horns of a goat, pulled itself out of the ground. The satyr smelled the air, then ran away into the thick of the woods and out of sight.

———————

TEMPLE OF GOULAUMX

TOMB CHAMBER

Reena, Roland and Zachary stand in awe as they stare in disbelief at the three newcomers standing in silence before them.

The tallest of the three seems to sense something unseen. He suddenly cried out, "the child has been born!"

"Are you certain of this, Fintazer," the other male asked.

Fintazer nodded briefly. "Yes Garex."

"The Star child is born," Garex proclaimed.

———————

GREENFIELD MEMORIAL HOSPITAL

DELIVERY ROOM

The nurse continued to clean the baby, but it was so silent in the room. It suddenly occurred to the nurse that the baby might not be breathing. Was it a trick of the light or was the child turning blue? The nurse suctioned the oral cavity of fluid. Usually, this was enough to trigger the baby's first breath. She called the doctor over. Did they used to smack a baby on the bottom to stimulate the child into crying? She didn't think that was still common practice, but perhaps a small pinch to the leg would be enough. She gave the child a small pinch just as the doctor came over to see what was wrong. The child opened its eyes revealing silver pupils. The baby screamed and the delivery room along with the entire south wing exploded.

ACKNOWLEDGEMENTS

My thanks and gratitude to:

Lawrence Fuchs, Jean Arbouet, Ruth Arbouet, The GoFundMe Team, Catherine McBrien , Damian Voerg , Daniel Holland, Chandler Owens , Roger Sherman, Jonathan Gladston , Gary Ostroff , Jackie Nichols, Harry McLaughlin, Kevin Arbouet, Carl Chiaramonte, Anne Marie and Stephen Raneri , Helene Harte James McBrien, Alan Spindel , L.J. Strong, John and Michelle Sikorski and John Celentano.

Your help has been invaluable to me, this book would have not come to fruition without your generosity, kindness and support. Again, thank you so much. I sincerely appreciate everything.

A special thank you to Mackenzie Grace Allison for her fantastic work as an editor and my wife Chery Russell-Arbouet who read the book numerous times who worked ceaselessly in the background and made me a better writer.

-Michael J. Arbouet

September 2018

Michael J. Arbouet is an author, indie film director and producer. He studied film at Long Island University. Gods, his first novel is based on his original screenplay. He lives on Long Island with his wife and two children where he is currently working on the sequel Gods book two. Follow @michaeljarbouet on Twitter. Or visit mikearbouet.com